# STORMY SEAS

## TWO THOUSAND GRUELING MILES BOOK THREE

### L.J. MARTIN

WISE WOLF BOOKS
An Imprint of Wolfpack Publishing
wisewolfbooks.com

STORMY SEAS. Text copyright © 2022 L. J. Martin
All rights reserved.
This is a work of fiction. All of the characters, organizations, publications, and events portrayed in this novel are either products of the author's imagination or are used fictitiously.

Cover design by Wise Wolf Books

ISBN 978-1-957548-11-1 (paperback) 978-1-957548-12-8 (hardcover)
978-1-957548-10-4 (ebook)

LCCN 2022948188

# STORMY SEAS

# 1

I SEE THEM COMING.

My Coach gun and my Sharps are in my room back at the Niantic Hotel, but no man would wander these streets without being heeled. I have both a new cap and ball Colt on my hip and a fine little .30-caliber belly gun in my trousers' pocket. Which I palm in my left hand as they near. Palm so it cannot be seen. Three of them. Slovenly fellas in bowler hats, soiled canvas miners pants, scuffed brogans, linsey-woolsey shirts, and unbuttoned wool waistcoats. Crooked noses and cauliflower ears testify to many dishonorable pastimes. Each of them wears a sidearm and pigstickers with foot-long blades and ivory—walrus—grips. The ivory is carved with a large 'W' which doesn't refer to the walrus they originated from but rather the Wallabys. Which I understand is the name the gang goes by. The knives are the calling cards of that Barbary Coast, Australian, Sydney Duck gang. And they don't look happy. Seems as a couple of months ago I'd shot five of their fellows dead as are the crabs boiling in front of a nearby café. I'd already learned the crabs taste much better than they smell cooking. Fact is, as the three Ducks stop in a semicircle only six feet from me, the boiling crab smells better than them.

"Hey, mate, you Jake Zane?" the biggest of them asks.

I rest my right hand on the butt of the Colt, but smile as I answer, "What's a jakezane?"

That seems to confound him for a moment, then he snarls, "You've got a smart mouth, mate. That could get a youngster like you skinned and fed to the wee fishes."

"Don't know no Jack Zane but do know that least two of you will be holed about dead center a'fore I go into the bay to feed the fish."

As I hoist the Colt just an inch or so to make sure it is riding light, I raise and cock the belly gun. The big man flinches as I do so.

"So, you *are* that back-shooting lowlife son of a she dog, Zane?"

"I done said, I never heard of no Jack Zane, so I suggest you go about your business and let a peaceful pilgrim be."

"I said Jake, not Jack."

"And I said leave me be. I've got a bit of a toothache and it's making me grumpy and wantin' to make some other fella, or three, hurt lots worse."

One of the others, a head shorter but built like a keg of whiskey, turns to the one that had been doing all the talking. "Hell's bells, Ian, this lout don't even know this Zane's right name. Let's keep poking around till we find the bugger."

The big one stands and eyes me a moment, with my belly gun centered on his prodigious gut, then seems convinced and nods.

He gives me a grin, showing a missing front tooth, spits on the boardwalk, then shrugs. "Sorry, mate, we heard this Zane was back in Frisco, and we got a bone to pick with him as he back-shot some good peace-lovin' friends of ours, my dear sweet brother among them."

"Then," I say, returning his smile, "I understand how y'all would be of a mind to do this Zane some harm. No harm done." I lower the belly gun, but don't uncock or pocket it. They spin on their heels and stroll away.

I didn't lie. I said I don't know any Jack Zane, and I don't. I casually retake my seat on the round wood piling that anchors the boardwalk. I'll soon have to head for my hotel, and a fancy supper I'll likely never in my life see the like of again. I'm the guest of honor at a shindig whose guests include the mayor of San Francisco, a few city councilmen, and some officers from the fort near the mouth of the bay.

My ma nor my sisters will never believe it. Me, a guest of honor!

It's near sundown, a heavy fog creeping in through the narrow opening that separates the Pacific from San Francisco and San Pablo Bay. Luckily, I still possess the coat my sis sewed from a Hudson Bay blanket, as a warm afternoon will soon turn bone rattling cold. Not the sharp bite of the Sierra which I've recently crossed, but a seeping chill that suddenly makes you wish for hearth and home.

I'm contemplating my next move, perched on a barrel on the Embarcadero, on the San Francisco waterfront—some call the Barbary Coast—in total awe of the stark, slightly undulating, forest in front of me. A barren, lonely sight. Eight hundred vessels, full three-masted ships, brigs, barks, and brigantines, schooners which I'm told are called goletas as you go farther south, and every other sort of vessel including steam driven side- and stern-wheelers that ply the bay and the Sacramento

River when crews can be found. The forest is of barren masts, a few seventy-five feet high, with crossarms, tar-covered stays, most stripped of all lines and sails as sailcloth and sound rope comes dear to argonauts who need tent cloth and the rope to secure it from ocean blasts of sodden wind. Few of them are manned, other than ferry boats, and those mostly by Chinese. The crews have all run off to the goldfields.

But a more practical use has been made of several ships, demasted and winched up onto shore, they now serve as saloons, bawdy houses, hotels, and shops of all varieties. A few skeletons lay on their sides in the mud, reminding one of a beached whale that's been stripped of skin and meat by scavengers, only these skeletons are mostly eastern oak ribs of ships stripped of all decking and planking. And behind the beached ship-saloons, as you climb up away from the muddy shore, is the dangdest sight a boy who's never seen a town bigger than St. Joe could imagine. Buildings have shot up three, four, and five stories high, and beyond the city are hills covered with white blisters...tents accommodating the thirty thousand the city has grown to over the last two and a half years. And it seems it's lucky a goodly number of two- and three-story buildings are there to be seen, as over half the city is now in charred ruins, some still smoking from a fire that must have lit the heavens while it burned two dozen blocks of clapboard buildings.

I learned the following from a recently established newspaper, *The Morning Post.*

Early in May a fifth Great Fire, only a few days following an earthquake, almost destroyed San Francisco. Another quake followed soon after the fire on May 15$^{th}$. The business district was inundated by flames as the fire leapfrogged from street to street. In less than a half day, eighteen blocks, over two thousand buildings, burned. Destruction was estimated over twelve million dollars. The fire destroyed all but the buried hulk of the ship *Niantic*. There was widespread belief that the fire was the work of gangs…the Hounds and Sydney Ducks. Loot from the fire was discovered in their quarters in Sydney Town. The fire started just before midnight, May 3rd, in a paint and upholstery store on the south side of Portsmouth Square and ravaged for half that day. James Welch of the Monumental Engine Company was killed along with four others when they were trapped in an iron-shuttered building during the fire. The flames were bright enough to be seen over one hundred miles away in Monterey. It was lucky hundreds didn't die.

A few lonely edifices, stone and brick, broken and scattered, still stand. If recent past holds true, they'll soon be toppled for rebirth as building material. Workmen, swarming like ants, are on them as soon as they cool. And as soon as the workmen earn passage and cost of a pick, shovel, and pan, they'll be like ants sprouting wings and flying away to the goldfields.

My ma told me when I signed onto a mule train, sitting shotgun, traveling nothing but game trails all the way from Lewistown on the Snake River to San Francisco, that we'd be lucky to make it. How right she was. Six of us rode out, and had I not hired another fella on near the end of the journey, I would have been the only one who rode in. And if I did make it, she assured me that a boomtown would be the death of me as every sort of thief and highbinder would be watching for a fella still picking the hay out of his hair and kicking his boots free of pasture patties.

And I guess that's me.

But I had no choice, as the locusts had eaten our

second crop down to a quarter inch below the plowed ground.

I guess I'm still a country boy, now on the shady side of seventeen, eighteen before I get back home, but I'm a different bumpkin than I was a little over two years ago when we set out from St. Joe. Like thousands, we set out on the Oregon Trail. First off, only a quarter into the trip, and me just turned fifteen, I became the man of the family. Pa died of the cholera leaving me with Ma and two sisters. Luckily Pa had hired on an escaped slave, Sampson, who was two and a half of me sizewise and even though mute—some son of a bitch of an overseer had cut out his tongue—he could handle a team, a Colonel Colt's sidearm, and about any chore needed doing.

I have put a sister sidearm to Sampson's, my double-barrel Coach gun, and a newly acquired Sharps to good use over the last twenty weeks, as the trip from Lewistown to San Francisco was fraught with wild things. Both mad critter and crazy men, some obviously savage, some with their savageness hidden behind a lying smile. They seem to pepper the trail like spiders awaiting a fly to tangle in its web. Red and white, men equally dangerous. I acquired my fine Sharps paper cartridge rifle gifted me by a dying man, a friend.

Our task was to transport a load of gold, the worth of which I could only imagine. Upon delivery Lord Willard Stanley-Smyth paid me a handsome sum, then as we'd left his stepson dead on the trail, his wife offered an even more handsome sum for me to return with charcoal and salt and pack his body and haul it back to San Francisco for a decent burial. He'd become a fine friend and saved me from donating my hair to the savage more than once and was the friend who with a note found in his belongings, gifted me the Sharps. The trip to fetch my friend's body was much easier as Lord Willard arranged for me to lead a platoon of California Guard to complete the task.

And we did go fetch his remains, without incident. It was my pleasure to do so as I'd hated leaving him shallow buried for the coyotes to dig. Luckily, they hadn't. Shallow buried as we were sure the same bunch of savages who'd felled him would soon again be upon us.

The result of all that has left me with some seven hundred and forty dollars in gold coin, two twenty-dollar gold pieces in each of my boots, six hundred and fifty in a money belt about my waist, and fifty in my pocket. It's a king's ransom for a country boy who'd feel rich as Midas with two ten-dollar gold pieces to rub together. But which will not last long in this city where an egg or oyster goes for a dollar as does a shot of whiskey. In other towns not plagued by gold fever, a half dollar can buy a steak, a half-dozen scrambled eggs, a pile of fried potatoes, biscuits, jam, and a bottomless cup of decent coffee. Of course, the sum in my pocket will last far less time if I fall victim to the Sydney Ducks and other lowlife but well-armed brigands who roam the city streets.

Near where I'm perched at the moment on the Barbary Coast, only near three months ago I was compelled to put the Sharps to work on a half-dozen brigands who had overpowered my employee, Tiny, and were seen loading the Stanley-Smyth bags of gold from the side-wheeler *Lawrence* onto a ketch. I was able to send five of the six to meet their maker from a distance of seventy-five yards or so—too far for their sidearms unless a lucky shot—and the other went to the city's fine jail. Lord Stanley-Smyth informed me I was again in his debt, and I'm due to return to his hotel for supper this very evening.

So, as things are, I'm looking to get back to the farm outside of Lewistown before my newfound wealth is consumed by the cost of living or a more heinous circumstance. That trip, if taken by sea, will land me at the mouth of the Columbia River, quite near where a young lady who has long had my attention, since we were neighbors on the wagon trip west, is said to reside. And near a number of riverboats plying that river and the Snake River which feeds it, and which leads within easy walking distance of our new family farm.

## 2

I stay seated, enjoying the scruffy dock workers going about their tasks, and the slick and sea-washed-clean seabirds—gulls and occasional pelicans hitting the water like six-pound cannonballs—until I figure I'd barely have time to wash up and dress.

The streets are busy, but luckily without a Sydney Duck in sight, as I weave through horsebackers, freight wagons, dray wagons loaded with kegs of beer, hacks, and the occasionally copper twirling his nightstick. All on the move as if they have a goal up ahead. Except for one gypsy looking chap cranking the handle on a music box playing a tune I think is *Rock of Ages.* Clever as it tugs at nearly everyone's heart strings. More for the sake of the skinny monkey dancing on a leash than for the cranker, I drop a nickel in his cup as I pass. I get a toothless smile from the gypsy and a polite nod.

The Niantic Hotel is a luxurious affair for so early in the life of a boomtown. A doorman eyes me carefully as I'm dressed more the drover than the dandy who'd normally attempt to walk past him as if he belonged.

But it seems the man in the royal purple cutaway coat, and tall top hat, remembers I had recently been accompanied by Lord Willard Stanley-Smyth, and gives me a nod after his short down-the-nose study. This will be only my second night in a hotel, in fact only my second night sleeping anywhere other than our former farmhouse on the Mississippi, my months on the Oregon Trail, or my time in the cabin that Sampson—the escaped slave Pa had hired to accompany us—and I'd built for Ma and my sisters near the Snake River. My Oregon Trail time was mostly in a hammock slung under our wagon. Of course, there was the many months on game trails and no-trail brush busting, sacked out in the open, from the Snake to San Francisco.

I fish in my pocket for the key to my room and have to smile as I work the lock. In all my few years the only lock I knew of was part of a small strongbox my pa kept our family papers in, and I'd never worked that lock.

Again, I smile as the room I enter—for just the use of the fella through whose eyes I was staring, me—is nearly the size of the cabin I'd built for the four of us. And more the target of my grinning glare is the bath I'd ordered, still steaming in a leather tub resting next to a bed wide enough to sleep three fat barkeeps lying flat on their backs. And all this is for me. I hurriedly strip away my trail-worn duds and sink full body into the water. In a little wire basket hanging on the tub's side is a bar of soap. Dang if it doesn't have even a whisper of a burn like the lye soap I'm accustomed to, and double-dang if it doesn't smell of lilac. I'm wondering if I'll have the whiff of a soiled dove trolling for customers when the water turns as cool as the outdoor baths Ma insists we face weekly back on the farm. I climb out to try on the fancy duds the Lord's lady has arranged to have spread out across the wide bed.

Just as I get dried off using a soft towel bigger than a horse blanket, there's a rap on the door. Wrapped in the towel I toe over and give some acknowledgment.

"All's fine here," I say, loud enough to be heard.

"Mr. Zane?"

"That would be me," I answer.

"Norman Peabody. I'm to serve as your valet while you dress for the affair."

"Valet?" I say, a little confounded.

"I'm to help you dress."

I have to shake my head at that one. "Dang if I ever needed help."

"Then you're skilled at tying a four-in-hand?"

As I barely knew what a four-in-hand was, I could not answer in the affirmative. Rather I inquired, "Are you alone, sir?"

"I am."

"Then please enter quickly as I'm just out of the creek and as God made me."

He's smiling as he enters. He's carrying a small leather satchel and a white porcelain pitcher, steaming with water.

"Good evening, sir," he says as he tosses me a pair of silk feet stockings and what I'd call the bottoms to a union suit, drawers, had they been wool rather than soft fabric, possibly cotton. They sport stirrups underfoot to hold the long leg-coverings down, and a button fly in case a visit to the privy necessary.

He then wraps another towel round my shoulder and positions a chair and invites me to plop down. Before I can complain he's lathering my face and I'm shaved with only one pause to strop the razor, then with the same razor and scissors nearly a year's growth of hair is on the floor.

Without another word I'm quickly adorned in matching trousers, a snow-white shirt, waistcoat, and coat as gray as a mourning dove with a spiffy blue four-in-hand silk puffy necktie. There's a looking glass on the door of a tall piece of furniture that serves as a clothes closet and I admire myself, right down to the shiny black brogans.

"This is a gift from the Lord," he says, as he drops a gold pocket watch, complete with chain, in the waistcoat pocket and droops the chain over and clips it onto the opposite pocket. And me used to telling time by how far the sun has traveled...

Again, before I can give a moan, he splashes some floral water over my cheeks so now I'm not only looking like a Boston politician but smelling like a French whore...not that I've had the pleasure of meeting either.

I give a low whistle. Dang if I don't look like a banker or maybe even a circuit judge.

"Very handsome, sir," my valet—that makes me laugh —says with an admiring look. Then he adds, "If you don't mind, I'm sure you've had little experience with such affairs as this, so may I offer some advice?"

"I'd be obliged," I say, and mean it as I'm more than a little apprehensive about showing my bumpkin side each time I turn around during the coming affair. In fact, my mouth goes dry each time I think on it.

The valet must have thought me a bumpkin even more so than I actually am. He grills me, teaches me, prods me, tests me and my fork selection, until I am a half hour late to my own party...which he quickly informs me is the proper way to make an impressive entrance.

I AM TAKEN ABACK by the sleeping room I am occupy, by the hot bath and valet, but none so much as by the room to which the valet guides me.

As we enter through double doors, each four feet wide by ten tall, the valet bides me to stop, instructs me to throw back my shoulders, stand as if at attention, and to meet every man's gaze strongly as if I was a potentate...and I feel obliged to do so as I recognize many potentate-level occupants from illustrations I've observed in *The Morning Post.*

Lord Stanley-Smyth bangs his and his wife's champagne glasses together, until I fear they'll smash, to get the crowd's attention, then walks over and embraces me with an arm around my shoulders.

His voice rings through the large room of at least a dozen round tables. "This young man is my friend, Jacob Zane. Jacob brought a valuable shipment all the way from near where the Snake River joins the mighty Columbia. A momentous task for an experienced mountain man, even more momentous for a young man yet to reach his majority. Beginning his trip riding as guard, along with five others, including my beloved stepson, Jacob was the only one to arrive. The others perished along the way from Indians, brigands, and accidents."

A round of applause from what must have been fifty attendees interrupts him, then he continues as I feel my cheeks redden.

"But this young man survived, and not only survived, but delivered that valuable cargo to me, then returned three hundred miles into the lair of the savage to bring my stepson's body back for a proper burial. Mr. Zane is a hero in the eyes of my wife and myself."

Then he leads the room in applause, and I redden even more.

When the crowd goes back to their drinks and snacks, the Lord leads me to a gray-haired gentleman with neatly trimmed—what I'd learn is called a Vandyke—facial hair with the waxed mustache portion curled up perfectly matching on each side. His silver hair is parted dead center, while his mustache and beard are pure white. He's dressed as fancy as me, except he sports a gold-mounted diamond stickpin centered in his silk four-in-hand, the stone the size of a green pea.

"Mr. Zane," the Lord says with seeming pride, "I'm proud to introduce you to California's Governor John McDougal."

The governor gives me a succinct smile, single pump handshake, then turns to others...probably San Francisco voters or donors.

Next I'm introduced to Marshal Robert G. Crozier, recently appointed. He's more cordial and knowledgeable. "You've had an eventful few months," he says, with a genuine smile. "If you're looking for work, I'm hiring city marshals. You'll get a fine copper badge, a sidearm, and four dollars a day if you can stay alive to collect." He laughs at that.

"I'm complimented, sir, that you'd consider me. But the fact is I have a mother and sisters—"

"Don't be so eager, young man," Lord Stanley-Smyth interrupts. "Keep up the great work, Crozier," he says to the marshal, then waves me over to a table featuring a large punch bowl which is surrounded by more than a half-dozen men and a couple of ladies.

"Captain Polkinghorn," the Lord calls out and a man turns and follows us away. He's beer barrel big with muttonchop sideburns that curl well beyond his ears.

"Luther," the Lord continues, "this is the young man I spoke of."

The big man eyes me up and down as if I'm a skinned pig ready to have my hams smoked, and would enjoy doing so, then asks, "You a seaman, young'un?"

# 3

"Somewhat a riverman, sir. But, no, I've not seen the sea until arriving in this city."

The big man turns to Stanley-Smyth. "Of no use to me, sir. I need men who are not afraid to mount a sixty-foot mainmast and furl a sail in a Force Five gale."

The Lord can see my hackles coming up, and asks, as if a challenge, "Jake?"

I step a little closer to the man he'd called captain; this time it's my neck going red, not my cheeks. "I learn fast, sir. I've packed mules, fought bit, bridle, bosal, breast collars, and britchin's on critters as wild as any piddly wind. The wind may blow hard, but it doesn't try to put you down and stomp you into a grease spot on the prairie, while savages are flinging arrows, trying to make you resemble a Swiss cheese. If I can fork a cayuse while facing hostiles at my front with wild rivers and lightning snapping at my rear, I guess I can learn what other men have been doing since before the Phoenicians."

The Lord is laughing. "Didn't I tell you, Luther. Call out for piss and vinegar and Jake will come running."

"All that don't get me to the Columbia and back," the captain grumbles.

"The Columbia?" I say. My tone completely changes.

"Lumber ship," Stanley-Smyth informs, knowing my hope to return to the Columbia and up it and up the Snake. "But you have to sign on for at least five-and one-half trips. It's my ship Luther captains, should that make a difference." Then the Lord adds, "First trip as a second mate, if you can stand the guff you'll take."

My interest is piqued. "And this pays?"

"A dollar a day and found and on a schooner plus one percent bonus on the profits of the trip for a common sailor. However, the second mate will receive two percent. First mate five and captain ten percent. It can be very lucrative as lumber is in high demand. If you become competent and move to one of our ships, the percentage is the same but the take usually higher as the cargo far greater…and I have two full three-masted ships, the *Orient Flyer* and *Oro del Pacifica*. The latter I bought in Mazatlán."

"How long," I ask, "will five trips take?"

Captain Polkinghorn answers. "Near seven hundred miles San Francisco to the Columbia. God willing, we'll make six knots or less against the current…heading northwest, but more than twice that speed on the downhill trip return."

"Downhill?" I ask.

"Normally with the wind and current. But fact is, just past the big river is the farthest we'll beat, and many lumber camps are much closer. More being rigged to load ships every week. When full we're with wind and current on our return."

"So, the Columbia is only five days, figuring sailing a

twenty-four-hour day, maybe a little longer than five, and half that return?"

"You cipher well, youngster. Maybe you can earn your keep. We'll be a day or two loading, maybe less than a day given a full load awaiting, and that much or more laying over here on our return. Always some repairs and stores to take on as well as off-loading."

I can't help but ask, "So, what happened to the last second mate?"

The captain furrows his brows. "Some of those logs weigh near a ton. Not a good idea to get between one and mast the same girth."

"I'd suppose not." I contemplate a moment, and all is silent.

Polkinghorn chuckles. "Probably best you stay ashore. Land is better suited for a plainsman." He nods and starts to turn away.

"So," I ask, "when do we leave?"

He turns back and gives me a glare. "You ain't hired yet, sonny."

"Sorry to overrule you, Luther," Lord Stanley-Smyth says, "but he's hired."

"Wait," I snap, "I have no interest in working where I'm not welcome. I can afford passage."

"No, sir," the Lord says. "I have plans for you, and it starts with you crewing on the *Windsong*."

"I plan to return to the Snake."

"If that's still your plan after you serve your five and a half voyages, so be it. But, young man, I don't see you breaking sod and praying the bugs don't eat your efforts for the rest of your life. You may see things my way by that time. Having another thousand or two in your trousers might influence your decision."

"So be it. We'll talk again in five voyages." I turn to the captain. "Does that suit your pleasure, Captain?"

"Lord Stanley-Smyth is the boss. But don't expect to be coddled."

"Never have been," I snap, a little too harshly. "Never will be if I have my way."

"Then get out of them fancy duds. You'll spend this night aboard. And every night until you're fed up with the salt in your nose and ears, and I'll wager that's within a fortnight."

"Wager how much?" Lord Stanley-Smyth asks, with a chuckle.

"Hold on," I say. "I'll not take a job where the boss profits from my failure. I prefer he profits from my success."

The Lord laughs again. "See, Luther, I told you he was smarter than the average sod breaker."

Even Polkinghorn smiles at that, but then he growls at me, "Get your rough duds and let's find a dry hammock for you."

It's not long before I meet him at the foot of the stairs, where he's chatting with the doorman. My bedroll with most all my belongings is over my shoulder, my Sharps and Coach gun rolled inside, my Colt again on my hip. I've left my new suit of clothes and tack stored with the hotel, hopefully safe as the cost is two dollars the month.

Polkinghorn eyes me skeptically, then shrugs.

"What?" I ask.

"You'll have little need for the armory."

"They are tools I know the use of, and when needed seem to be the only tool to do certain work."

He shrugs again, so I guess that endorsement is enough.

So, it's a new life and endeavor for me, even if, I figure, for a little more than two months, at the most.

———

THREE COAL OIL lamps are all that lights the deck of the *Windsong*. I know Captain Luther Polkinghorn is not happy about being forced to hire me, and as we walk in silence down to the harbor, I make up my mind to quickly dispel any of his apprehensions.

After a long quiet walk to nearly the end of the wharf, he pauses and points to a three-masted ship at the end of the wharf. Beyond it, in the bay, a number of ships—dozens, still float. They have been abandoned by argonauts.

"That's her?" I ask, as I study the vessel seemingly ten times as long as my Oregon Trail wagon and team, and thousands of times the weight. I take a very deep breath and let it out slowly. I'm wondering if I've stepped out of the storm and into the maelstrom?

# 4

"That's the *Windsong*. She's one hundred fifty feet, two hundred fifty tons loaded lightly. She's built for coastal trade, shallow draft for a ship of her beam and length."

"Sir," I interrupt. "I thought schooners were only two masted?"

"No. Number of masts are not the determination. Her sails are fore and aft of the mast, not square-rigged, thus a schooner. And this one be a topsail schooner. Two square-rigged sails are atop the foremast, if the wind favors they'll help her turn in two lengths, but that's the extent of it. She's quick to respond to the helm, so rigged, so needed when shoals, rocks, and sandbars are the threat as they are to any coastal."

I clear my throat, trying to determine the proper way to address this new boss of mine. I know we didn't get off to the best start. "Captain, may I say—"

"Say any damn thing you want, younger. I got skin thick as a walrus. That said I'll knot your head should you not be respectful."

"Sir, you know I know little or nothing about the sea and sailing, but you should know you'll not meet another more willing to learn. I, too, have thick skin, so no matter my relationship with Lord Stanley-Smyth, please treat me as you would any new hand. No matter how loudly you might yell at me, I'll listen and learn and have no hard feelings."

He chuckles. "Never doubt my treating you as every other sogger aboard. You may be surprised at how loud I can yell and curse those who might cause us a few seconds tardy. It ain't got nothing to do with you, it's the job, son. The job. I take a job of work damn serious and so should you. You'll learn fast or likely take a peek at Davy's locker...and maybe give your regards to Neptune."

"Davy's locker? Neptune?"

Again he chuckles. "Yep, at the bottom of the briny unforgiving sea. A place you don't want to visit. By the way, don't expect the crew to accept a know-nothing as second mate. You'll find resentful the order of near every day."

"I'll earn respect, a day at a time."

"You've got sand, I'll give you that much."

I follow him up the gangway, then from bow to stern as he points out the intricacies of the ship. Between each of her three masts is forty feet distance, and two hatches —hold covers—each thirty feet by ten openings, into which a lift of lumber, a forty foot or even longer log can be easily inserted, then when the holds are filled, the decks can be loaded forward of the rear deckhouse which accommodates cookshack, crew, and officer's quarters. Atop that is the wheelhouse. The first and second mate enjoy two bunks at the rear of eight, separated only by hanging canvas, that makes up the rest of the crew. Then comes the galley with a small kitchen to the larboard. A stack pierces the hull through a gasket carved from soapstone, so a red-hot stack won't set the hull afire. The most aft cabin is the captain's quarters with a hatch and ladder leading up into the wheelhouse. Sixteen of us, plus captain, to handle well over two hundred tons of vessel, empty. I'm accustomed to handling four oxen of over a thousand pounds each, this is definitely a step up.

Eight of the common seamen and the first mate are ashore so I meet only four as I'm shown to my bunk. Others are on watch.

Terrill Taggart, who says call him Tag, seems near my age and is thin as a harpoon. Sour John Posterwick, is thin as a harpoon, seeming deserving of his nickname. Jack Pyle looks to be half-African and smiles enough for all of them. And to my great surprise, Su Lee Hong, an Asian woman who the captain quickly explains is cook and mends sails and keeps garments in the slop chest repaired and in good order. She only comes under my arm high, sizewise, but sticks out her bony hand and shakes like a man. To my additional surprise she has the grip of a blacksmith and calluses to boot.

The captain points out my bunk—not a hammock to my pleasure—then leads me into his stateroom. The width of the ship, it is palatial compared to other quarters.

He explains, "On the normal vessel the crew would be forward, in the forecastle, with the second mate...and only other officers aft. We value a long deck, so forward is as flat as the builders could construct her. We occasionally even load lumber alongside the wheelhouse, although it's a fool's errand as the higher the weight the more likely to broach with this shallow draft...no keel to speak of. Loading too high is to risk the ship for a few extra dollars."

The captain's bunk is half-again as much the width of others, and gimballed to stay level with the ship's sway. A desk and chart table fill the open area, and a closet with a thick door sports a lock the size of my palm, he explains the ships valuables including arms are stowed behind the locked door. Then he adds, "Your armory will be stored inside. We want no accidents with the crew."

It's my turn to shrug.

He gives me a hard look. "This is the last time you'll be in this stateroom unless ordered, understand?"

"Clearly."

"Clearly, sir."

"Yes, sir. Clearly, sir." I notice he says ordered, not invited.

He hands me two thick, leather-bound, well-worn books. *Mariner's Guide, Techniques, Skills and Knots for all the Seven Seas* and *The "Intelligent Mariner": Nathaniel Bowditch, the Science of Navigation, and the Art of Upward Mobility in the Maritime World.*

"You'll want to know these, cover to cover."

"Yes, sir."

"We sail with the tide in the morning."

And he meant morning. Seems the tide turns at five o'clock which means we arise at four to prepare to weigh anchor and set sail. I quickly determine that I am to learn a whole new lexicon; terms onboard ship are as unlike terms on a farm or wagon train as a porpoise is from a donkey. I also meet the four formerly absent crewmen, who'd returned in the night. I have yet to meet the others.

I've read many books, prior to setting out on the Oregon Trail, and each night on the trail under the tutelage of my sainted mother and enjoyed most. The six-inch-thick tomes of small print I'd been handed, do, however, give me pause.

Boston Bob is a brindle-headed lout, red hair but blond beard, who seems to think it an amusing talent to talk in rhyme. Rufus Goatherd has a Cockney accent and speaks almost as foreign were it Swahili. Baldur Olafsson, from a place called Iceland, carries the nickname Baldy although he has a mass, a mess, of straw-colored hair. Last but far from least as he fills the passageway and would frighten a bull buffalo with his tattooed face, is Akamu Ka Ana Ana, a Sandwich Islander, known as Kanakas, who the rest call Mumu. I learn all this, pulling the canvas aside to make small talk with the crew, while we quickly dress.

As soon as my feet hit the deck the captain waves me over and introduces me to First Mate Lawrence McGillicutty. It's hard not to stare as McGillicutty has a puckered scar from ear to the dimple on his chin and the left side of his mouth and face sags a half-inch lower than the right. And his welcome is about as ugly.

"So, you're the lubber who's the pet of the owner. You'll be Jack Nastyface aboard."

"And that means?" I ask.

"You'll sir me just as you do the captain," he growls.

"And that means, sir?" I repeat.

"I'll not take you to raise, lubber. Go forward and observe...don't talk, don't interrupt, just watch."

"Yes, sir," and I do. And watching an experienced crew set sail and raise anchor then the captain and first mate and all-hands-on-deck thread one hundred fifty feet and over two hundred tons through a plethora of dead-in-the-water ships, boats, and ferries is a sight to behold. An order is shouted to those in the shrouds above, those on deck, and the sailor on the wheel, with almost every breath. I quickly understand why these men are proud of what they do, and slow to embrace a novice. Watching a man high on the foremast, set sail on the square sails, I quickly surmise a mistake might likely be a man's last, and a drastic error might be the end of the ship. My first taste of ship handling convinces me it's certainly an art as well as a profession. I find no trouble keeping my mouth shut.

I have the strong feeling, deep in my marrow, that the Lord has done me no favor elevating me above the common sailors. I'm reminded of being thrown into the head of the family when my father passed from the cholera, only two months into the most difficult task my family ever encountered.

Only now I was cast into a job so foreign from a wagon train with a language I must learn while doing, and it seems a little like learning to tie your boot while at a dead run.

I do ask Boston Bob, while the captain and McGillicutty are together in the wheelhouse, what a Jack Nastyface might be?

"He's a man who all aboard hate, a man probably soon to be bait."

"Thanks," I say, but don't mean it. I think I'd as soon not know.

5
---

I don't think a man meets my eye, other than the first mate and captain, and both of them seem to have perfected the disdainful sneer.

But not long after we breech the narrows and have the Farallon Islands in sight off the larboard, I could care little what anyone thinks or does, or even if they, or I, live. I'm hanging over the taffrail, chumming the fish until I feel my gut is about to come up with the bile. This, at least, gets a smile from the first mate.

As he follows me and shoves me into my bunk, with the admonition, "You'll be up before the sun, ready for what the day brings…or a boot to your butt and you'll wave farewell sinking in the foamy brine. Understand?"

"Yes…yes, sir," I mumble, then retch again but all I gain is a bad taste in my mouth.

It's after midnight before I sleep, and well before dawn when I'm awakened by a rough hand.

"Mr. Zane," I'm startled by the tattooed face of the Kanaka. So big it looks like a brown dinner plate, painted with odd dark designs, leaning over me.

"Time to fall out?" I ask weakly.

"Aye. Burgoo, hot and sweet and she'll be settling your gut, should you keep it down."

"Thank you. And your name again?"

"I is called Mumu."

"Thank you, Mumu."

I quickly pull on my rough clothes and am met at the table in the galley by grunts and perfunctory salutes. I'm directed to sit with the crew. A walkway, and hanging worn sail, separate our table from that of the captain and first mate. Although the captain is not in attendance and I'm told he often eats in his stateroom. Only ten of us are at the table, so I presume the others are on deck.

A lively conversation is carried on by the nine members of the crew at the table. I soon learn that when weather even slightly worsens, we'd be two equal shifts or watches, with nine men always topside, and often the call "all hands" rings out. Burgoo is nothing as special as its name—oatmeal, salt, and sugar. As common as the moving floor, deck, under my feet is uncommon. But now it's an easy roll as we've left the current and rough water roaring in and out of the relatively narrow opening of the huge harbor that is San Pablo and San Francisco Bay. I feel better with the cool breeze topside.

Sour John Posterwick is the most senior of the common sailors, and Captain Polkinghorn assigns him to be my teacher, which pleases him as it gets him out of his duties for a while but displeases him as he gets the wrath of the other sailors for his easy assignment. He seems pleased when I begin calling him Professor Posterwick rather than Sour John. It is the first smile I get from anyone on board. We start at the stern taffrail and work our way forward to the bowsprit, concerning ourselves with the lines and stays, then back with the masts, booms, gaffs, and sails. A rope is not a rope, but a line, and a line covered in tar is also not a rope or a line, but a stay, as it secures the various fixed appendages of the lady, primarily the massive masts. The ship is a her. The stays are stiff and in place, while lines move, like halyards that run through winches to hoist and lower, tighten and loosen against the wind, sails. Tighten to remove luffing. Loosen to remove strain. And run through block and tackle to load and unload cargo. When we come about—turn—we have to realign sails to catch the wind, and as second mate I am expected to work right along with the crew. I soon learn the use of the sailor's friend—cork sewed into canvas in a ring, to be flung to the sea if needed to follow a man overboard. I eye them carefully, two on the starboard and two on the larboard—coming to be called the port—and both forward and aft. I hope I'll never see the need of them.

And I am informed I am expected to take the crews complaints to the first mate and captain, but only if I feel them warranted. First loyalty to captain and ship, second to the crew. It seems a tenuous position to be in, but it is a time-honored one and who am I to question.

The watch goes quickly and ends with my head swimming. We are to work four on and four off with two, two-hour dogwatches. It works out so a man can get one six-hour break a day for a decent sleep. Again, who am I to question. I ask about the Sabbath and am informed that our runs are so short the Sabbath is not celebrated on any Sunday, but whenever a man chooses to do so, if he does.

The noon meal is a mishmash of something called dandy funk; broken biscuits which reminds me of hardtack, and whatever bits and pieces of leftovers are handy, all slathered in molasses. By the amount of molasses generously lathered on, I presume there's a hogshead barrel aboard that has to be regularly refilled. I'm pretty sure our little cook, Su Lee Hong, would never get a job at the Niantic. Come to think of it, in my many hours reading while crossing the prairie, I learned that women were generally considered bad luck aboard ship. Sour John informs me that women often sail with their husbands, and Su Lee sleeps in the captain's stateroom and has since before Sour John had signed aboard over a year ago.

So I presume the woman-aboard thing was merely superstition, at least I pray so. And I presume Su Lee's obligations involve more than slopping the crew. I say slopping as so far the fare is served more like I slopped our hogs than my ma set a table. At least there's plenty of it.

Before I return to duty, the wind has freshened enough that the ship begins to heel, or lean over. What had been a relatively flat deck is now beginning to angle steeply. I am a little surprised to learn that we are sailing only forty-five degrees off the wind in our face. Sour John explains the lift, or driving force of the wind, is caused by the shape of the sail. It has me scratching my head, but it is not to be the only thing to confound me about sailing and the sea, and the very intricate workings of a sailing ship.

I must dig into my books.

I am pleased that the rise and fall of the ship no longer bothers me. I'd had nightmares about continual sickness on board, and Polkinghorn's prognosis that I wouldn't last ten days. I'll die before I give up.

As my pa, God rest his soul, often instructed me, a man has no back-up in him.

Why, I have no idea, but the wind suddenly shifts and

we heel from starboard to larboard, and amidships Mumu wheels backward, his arms windmilling, and goes over the rail. He resembles a walrus tumbling over a seaside rock.

Almost in unison, more than one man yells, "Man overboard!" and charges to the rail but merely watches. I hit the rail, and dragging a sailor's friend with me, dive into the brine. It is slightly reassuring that I hear Polkinghorn scream the order, "Come into the wind. Jolly boat launched." The ship carries two small twelve-foot boats, each with two pairs of oar locks and a mast and sail if needed.

Mumu is already seventy-five feet in the wake, but I swim as fast as I know how, dragging the sailor's friend on its line behind. As I near the big man, I realize how dangerous my situation is. I look over my shoulder to see the ship turning into the wind. She'd stop with sails now acting as a break, not a driving force. But even then, it takes a distance for a many ton ship to come to a halt.

Mumu is no swimmer, and is beating the water like a beaver slapping the pond with his flat tail, warning of oncoming danger. Before I reach him he disappears, so when at that spot, I dive. The Kanaka has a full head of shoulder length, thick black hair, and I'm able to get a handful and kick and stroke with the other for the surface.

I suck a deep breath when surfacing…and it's a good thing as I am quickly sucking water, not life-giving air, as the big man, all clawing feet, ham-size hands, and tree-trunk-size arms and legs, tries to climb aboard me.

And down I go, under a desperate walrus-size mass of clamoring violence.

## 6

I BRING MY FEET UP AND KICK WITH ALL MY MIGHT, knowing I must fight clear of the huge man, and spring away and luckily pop to the surface. The *Windsong*, even with luffed sail, is still disappearing into the mist.

The huge Kanaka is beating the surface as if he'll find something to claw himself atop of, but I realize that something cannot be me. The jolly boat is still a hundred yards away, coming as fast as four men can work the oars...but won't reach Mumu in time as he's again disappearing under the foam.

The sailor's friend and I were separated when he drove me below the surface, but I see it only twenty feet away, and stroke for it. I sling it back to Mumu's last position, but again, he's gone below. Stroking back, I dive again, and again find a handful of hair. I drag him to the surface only this time I kick away before he tries to use me for a ladder. I only have to fling the sailor's friend six feet to reach him, and do, and he clings to it like a remora to a shark's belly...or so I've read, but hope never to see up close and personal. He's upchucking water, snorting like a bull buffalo in heat, and spitting water like a San Francisco fire company hose, but remaining topside.

I stay far enough from him he has no chance to use me as a flotation device, until the jolly boat skims up between us, and hand over hand I grasp along an oar and am hoisted aboard as others try and haul Mumu over the far side oarlock. It takes three sailors to do so and damn near capsizes us.

Boston Bob is the man who's helped me and gives me a slap on the back. "That was the act of a good fellow, I'll write a song and we'll give you a bellow."

I can't help but reply, "And I'm glad to be aboard," then cough, then add, "the boat's safety I'll hoard." He gives me a look like I'm stealing his thunder, then laughs, takes his seat, and while Mumu and I cling thankfully to the bottom of the jolly's hull, they stroke for the *Windsong*, now nearly out of sight in the mist.

It's a rope ladder to the deck, and a greeting I don't appreciate from ugly-scarred First Mate Lance McGillicutty, as Captain Polkinghorn stands back, fists firmly planted on his hips. First to me, he rumbles, "You had no order to go after that man. There'll be no grog for you for a week," then to Mumu, "You clumsy damn oaf, I knew when I signed you, I knew that you'd be a burden, too damn big to move lightly. It's two weeks dry for you and holystoning the deck when not pulling line." All Mumu can do is nod.

McGillicutty mumbles to the captain as they walk away, "It'll likely take a day to make up the time, damn them."

The captain seems lost in thought, then speaks loud enough so all can hear. "Lay on sail, we'll make straight for Humboldt Bay with the wind at our back. The *Sea*

*Shrike* is abaft and will leave us in her wake before we fill sail, and we'll need to beat her to the load, so it's all hands. Set the studding sails." Then he turns to where Mumu and I had plopped our butts on a deck box, me still trying to catch my breath, Mumu trying to clear the water from nose, ears, and worse, lungs.

"You two have cost us a sure berth at the Humboldt mill. You'll pull a double watch."

"Yes, sir," I manage. So much for playing the hero.

McGillicutty snaps at both of us, "And you'll both go aloft to hoist—"

"No, mate," Polkinghorn stops him short. "It's no time to break the lubber in. We'd just have to do another rescue and the load is more important."

As they walk away Sour John walks over and lays a hand on my shoulder. "You've cut a notch of good with your quick work. The crew will think more kindly of you."

"I moved without thinking. Just did what I thought—"

"You did what needed doing and did it well."

I am getting a little embarrassed, so I change the subject. "What's a studding sail?"

"The two square-rigged topsails will be backed by a duplicate sail, to catch the wind spilled and give us an extra push. It's high and dangerous work and the captain has my respect for not sending you aloft. He gets a notch on the good side as well."

Later, after our double watches are complete and we've cleaned up a bowl of beans and we're sopping the juice and molasses with the treat of fresh bread, one of Su Lee's specialties, Mumu speaks of his near-death experience for the first time.

"I owes you, Mr. Zane."

"You don't owe me a thing, Mumu."

"No. I owes you. My life now your life, Mr. Zane."

"Pardon me?"

"My life save by you. My life, now yours. You ask, I do."

I have to laugh at that. "If you do for me it's because I'd do the same for you."

"You ask, I do."

I again have to chuckle at that, even though it seems he is deadly serious. Maybe that's a Kanaka thing, a life saved is a life owed? I fall asleep easily and get my three hours without a dream, or the nightmare I could have easily had.

———

AS THE SUN rises I can see the ship the captain had called the *Sea Shrike*, far aft of us and traveling just a few degrees west of north, while Polkinghorn has our course nearly seventy degrees west of north, or 290 degrees on the compass. I am working alongside Sour John, him again acting as professor as I learn to mend line, another skill that will come handy in the barn.

"John, why are we pulling away from the coast?"

"The coast of California is north by northwest, and the current, she runs southerly at three knots or so. We'll lose time for a while but when our latitude is near that of Humboldt, Cap'n will bring us near due east and we'll be crossing the current, not fighting her head-on."

"I notice the *Sea Shrike* is schooner-rigged but without the two square sails atop her foremast?"

"Aye, that's a bald-headed rig. You're getting an eye for things, Mr. Zane. She'll beat us near the wind, but we'll leave her in our foam with the wind at our back, even twenty or thirty degrees off, and God willing, beat her to the mill on the Humboldt. We'll be sipping the syrup out of the bay's oysters on the way home."

"And the distance, San Francisco to Humboldt?"

"Three hundred fifty as the gull flies, but we'll do closer to five hundred and, with the wind favoring, still be taking on logs and milled timber when the *Sea Shrike* limps in. She'll be a week more taking on cargo while we're counting our coin back in San Fran."

The mountains are beginning to swell on the eastern horizon, and I am told Humboldt Bay is dead ahead, but we can't enter unless with the high tide as a shallow sandbar blocks the entrance.

By the time we near the entrance a low fog occludes all but the high mountains behind, with a wind abaft, but softened, we creep toward the narrow opening. I swear I hear the hull scrape sand but the captain charges forward. And as we enter, as if welcoming us, the fog lifts and I can see the long expanse of the bay, maybe three miles wide and to my surprise many miles long.

Jack Pyle and I are tending a foresail halyard, preparing to come about. While awaiting the order, I stared at the distant shoreline and realized it is lined with savages.

7

"They hostile?" I question him.

"Ain't they all. The captain will have gifts for them. The loggers have a well-armed guard at all times."

"Is there a village?"

"This bay was only discovered a little over a year ago, and that from the landside. She couldn't be seen from seaward."

"This tribe have a name?" I ask.

"Wiyots. They's lots of villages around the bay and up along the Elk River. The loggers had a run-in or two with them and a few crews went up river and didn't come back so's they brought in the California Guard, and as I heard it they wiped a couple of villages out… women, children, anything moving. So as I hear it they fight shy of you white folks now."

That makes me remember that I am told Jack is half-Carib or some dang thing from down in the sugar islands. Half Black, so said Sour John. So I merely nod.

He continues, "Seems them clubs and bows and

arrows ain't much against Colonel Colt's and Mr. Aston's or Mr. Ame's fire breathers."

"I'd guess you never had to dodge a sky full of arrows?"

"Nope, and don't plan to."

"Don't underestimate them. These folks, at least the ones inland, have done right well for many generations with the bow and arrow. I learned to respect them."

"Man does with what he has to do with," Jack says, and we are given the order to come about.

As we come hard a'larboard I can see a small, sleek schooner moored a hundred yards offshore, and a line running from her fore or mizzenmast to a tower of logs ashore. Another pair of lines leads away from the mast into the bay, and as we near I can see there are four pilings to which the schooner is secured on the landside. She is fixed tightly with at least four anchors, and I can soon see why. As I eye the mountain behind, clear-cut for a couple of hundred yards in a semicircle, I can see the drag marks of a hundred logs and beyond a tree, at least one hundred feet tall is starting its descent, gaining speed, toppling, until it slaps into the mountain raising a cloud of dust and sawyer's trash and then is quickly swarmed on by a half-dozen loggers who began stripping branches away. A six-up of mules stands patiently just downslope as two loggers chain traces to the log. By the time we drop anchor, just inside the little schooner, the tree is being quartered with three teams, each on eight-foot-long crosscut saws.

Some logs are floated to a nearby mill—driven on a sluice of water coming at a steep angle out of the forest above—and reduced to timber, and it's then milled again to shorter two-by and four-by rafters and posts, some seemingly as short as ten feet. It would seem not a foot of hold and deck will be spared a load. Full logs forty feet in length, probably for piers and bridges, jobs requiring the strongest of support, and other sawn lumber for general building.

And all, other than the mill powered by falling water, are powered by a herd of at least fifty mules. It's an anthill of men and animals, swarming in different directions with different pursuits.

"Mr. Zane!" my concentration on the work ashore is interrupted by the captain's yell. I think myself in trouble due to my lollygagging at the shore work, but there is no fire in his eyes as he waves me aft of the mainmast to the wheelhouse. I hustled to join him.

"I presume you cipher?" he asks before I reach his side.

"As good as the next man," I answer.

"And your penmanship?"

"Clear as a cloudless sky," I say, with some pride.

"Then to my stateroom, fetch quill, inkwell, and the ledger they rest on. You're ashore to count the load from that end. McGillicutty will do a count as we take aboard our load. If you value your grog or more than bread and water in the galley you'll match his count…exactly. Launch the jolly boat and pick a man to accompany you and man the oars."

"Mine will be accurate, sir. Can't speak for Mr. McGillicutty."

"You are a sassy lad. See that your mouth doesn't overload your ego."

"Yes, sir."

I chose Mumu to go along. Should a grizzly bear roar down out of the forest, Mumu will likely be his equal.

We are greeted by a man with shoulders as wide as ax-handles and a full head of hair and beard, a color I first thought blond but discovered is red. The blond is sawdust and wood chips covering head, shoulders, and forearms. He meets me with an outstretched hand. A hand so calloused it resembles the bark on the nearby stack of logs.

"Red Sorenson, this is my outfit, and you'd be?"

"Jake Zane, second mate, and my man on the oars is Mumu."

"Aye, I have seen Mr. Mumu about before. So, you're to mark the ledger?"

"I am, sir."

"Find a stump for your rump and as soon as your captain gives us a wave, we'll haul away." And with that he gives me his back.

We do as he suggests, where we have clear view of the hoists and other apparatus for hoisting the logs and bundles of sawn lumber and sending them the near seventy-five yards out to the *Windsong*, which has been positioned between shore and the lumber camp schooner. I soon to learn this is called a trapeze. Aboard the *Windsong* I can see the crew busily positioning the main booms from both main and mizzenmasts, raised nearly halfway up the masts they'll serve to move the logs into position and lower into the hold or stack on deck. It's obvious with the first log run down the line, suspended at both ends, that shore and ship crew are well experienced with the process. The last bundle of sawn lumber is in place on the deck just as the sun disappears into the fog, then the orange lobe drops into the sea, or so it seems. I know there is a sandbar between us and the distant horizon but occluded by the mist and fog it is unseen. My log has a page full of four marks each crossed, indicating five logs or a lift of sawn lumber.

A Chinese youth, a half-dozen years my junior, keeps

giving us, and more often the lumberjacks, drinking water, but we've not eaten since a bowl of oats twelve hours before, so it is with a succinct handshake we bid Red Sorenson good day and row back to our ship and home…and hopefully a full bowl and cup of grog.

As we down a generous bowl of hot elk stew, the captain stops at our table. "My compliments, Mr. Zane. Your total matches that of Mr. McGillicutty's." Then he turns to all of the crew, other than the two men standing watch on deck. "Gentlemen, eat hardy. You'll sleep for two and a half hours. High tide is near the witching hour, and we'll be broaching the shallows, with luck, exactly then. We're four feet less draft, so it has to be near exact. If we make it clean without having to dump half our deck load, you'll all have a chance to bleed the monkey."

The men cheer. I knew not why, but join in. As the captain returns to his stateroom, Sour John sees I am a bit perplexed.

"It's an extra cup of grog, Mr. Zane. Technically it refers to a man sneaking a straw into a keg of grog, but in this instance it's the captain's way of saying we'll earn a bit more."

I gave him a smile in return. "And all we have to do is get a ship drawing four feet less than scraping bottom on the way in, to get safely out."

"Aye, that's all."

"And if we don't?"

"I done saw you swim like a porpoise, and should we broach thanks to taking an incoming wave in a narrow passage with a shallow bottom and a maximum load, it may serve you well."

# 8

McGillicutty posts Sour John out on the bowsprit armed with a heaving line. A two-pound lead weight is secured to the end of the narrow half-inch rope, which John slings, as far as possible, ahead of the ship as we creep forward at no more than one knot or maybe a little more. Thankfully the wind is nearly sixty degrees off our starboard, or we'd have had to wait for a favoring direction. I can't help but wonder why the captain doesn't wait another twelve hours for the next high tide, in the light, but I'll not second-guess a man who's forgotten more about his task than I'll likely ever know.

Sour John's job is to test the depth by slinging the weight ahead of our course, a task accomplished as much by feel as to when the weight strikes bottom, as much as sight. In the floating fog and silence—we're chastised if we breath too hard as it's critical the man on the wheel, far aft, can hear Sour John's every report. It's as eerie and nearly as frightful as wandering into a deep, dark copse of evergreens knowing a wounded grizzly is stalking you. We're cursed by a sliver of a moon and that is rapidly being sheltered by the layer of fog that seems to haunt the sand strip that blocks bay from ocean.

And scream Sour John does, "Three fathoms, hard abaft!"

And men jump to dropping sail, but one hundred fifty feet of heavily laden ship does not stop on a wish and a prayer. And by the count of ten we're thrown forward as our prow plows into the bottom, only two fathoms below our waterline…luckily seemingly sand and not hull-and-timber-ripping rock. It's a grind we hear and feel, not a gut-wrenching crack.

But the striking of the sand bottom is not the worst of it as, when we grind to a stop, the wind heels us even farther to the larboard, the lee side, and, with the snapping of taught hemp line used to secure the load, several lifts of lumber tumble over the rail, smashing the rail to splinters in the process.

The captain yells, "Grappling hooks and line, launch the jollys!" but he is a few seconds late with the order as McGillicutty is already on the starboard jolly, and Boston Bob and Rufus Goatherd are yelling at me to follow to the larboard boat.

The ship is heeling to the right, but with dumping much of starboard deck load and weight, she rights herself and now leans into the wind to the left, the windward or weather side. The three of us are jumping from lift to timbers to lift, when they start to edge over the larboard rail. We have to leap and tumble to keep from going overboard with the top loads on the right but recover and soon have the jolly boat suspended over a thrashing sea as lifts of lumber and logs begin to drift away with what remains of the incoming tide. Luckily, we're nearing high tide, so the drift is very slow.

However, the tide will soon turn, and logs and lifts could be lost forever drifting out to sea.

To my surprise, as we unhitch and row away from the ship, I hear Sour John yell out, "Three fathoms!" and the captain shout the order to reset the main and mizzen and presume with the lightening of the ship's load she'll now skim over the sandbar.

I can't help but wonder if we'll be left behind.

Then Goatherd yells something—I can't understand his Cockney accent—and Bob repeats, "You're on the hook, Mr. Zane." And I understand I'm to throw the hook to capture floating log or lift of lumber, and after four or five minutes of the able work of Bob and Rufus on the oars, we're within pitching distance of a lift, and I stand, take a moment to catch my balance, and make a couple of swinging three sixties with the hook and easily make the twenty-five-feet distance to hook a lift of lumber amidships, then take a few half hitches on the forward stanchion.

"We'll have to move it aft," Bob says, and I loosen it and struggle between them to perform the same half hitches on the aft stanchion as they maneuver the boat around to begin to chase the *Windsong*. As we're still against the current, it's a slow and difficult trip. I'm not surprised to have us pass the other jolly boat, with McGillicutty on the hook, hard after their own load.

I'm a little surprised we can make any headway towing a twelve-foot-long, four-foot-diameter lift of four-by-twelve timbers. But we do, and after a half hour of hard rowing, the current has stilled, and thank God, will soon be assisting us.

It's another half hour before we sight the rigging of the *Windsong*, anchored in the distance.

We deliver our load and change oar men. Mumu and

young Taggart, Tag to us, take the place of Rufus and Bob, and now we're pulling against the outgoing current but make time as we're not towing.

It's noon before we've recovered all we can find, sweat now soaking clothes and running off our foreheads. As we're collecting lumber one of our competition ships, the *Sea Shrike*, enters the harbor. But he'll either have a week's wait in Humboldt or be off to find another mill more northerly, as we damn near picked this one clean.

The winds favor us on our run back to San Francisco, even arriving on an incoming tide. I'm given a twenty-four-hour leave ashore and as I'm strolling down the gangplank I'm met by a young messenger and find myself invited back to the Niantic Hotel to dine for lunch with the good Lord. I presume he wants to learn if I've taken kindly to the sea.

Hell, I don't know myself as of yet. I do know my shoulders are still in knots from helping row to recover lost lumber, my hands are blistered, my mind is swimming from all I've learned, but the fact is I'm smiling a lot and pleased with myself.

I have my sea legs, and other than that first day, it seems seasickness is in my past. And I've met some fine fellows and learned a million helpful tasks and half-dozen sea chanteys.

Living aboard ship, with its strict discipline and structured authority is interesting to me, new to me, and something I never thought I might actually enjoy. Your whole world is suddenly within one hundred fifty feet with one man who, it seems, is as powerful as God...in fact is god on board the vessel.

I'm thinking I'll have to take a much bigger bite of sea

life before I call it more than a casual pastime and a short learning experience.

Time will tell, and four and a half more promised excursions.

I have four hours to kill before my luncheon, so find the seashore version of a sutler, a mercantile which sells the folderol of the sailor of the sea, not the plains. A chandlery is my quest. I don't have far to walk, as just across the wharf is a sign, the Able Seafarer. I've watched Sour John use a marlinespike and want a folding knife that will hold an edge and fit in a pocket, hopefully one with a small folding spike. It is a tool I can use around the barn almost as much as around the deck, so its purchase is not confessing to the want of a life at sea. I also want a knit hat I can pull down over my ears to keep the night sea chill at bay, and in addition I buy a jaunty straw with a narrow upturned brim that came all the way from Panama. I have other needs as well, and eight and a half dollars later I am pleased with my new gear.

I have learned from Captain Polkinghorn that my share of the load will likely exceed one hundred dollars, which will add nicely to my growing poke.

Now, to remember my manners as it is time to wander up the hill to lunch.

Of course, it is only a half block before I come face-to-face with three of the same ugly Sydney Ducks, the Wallaby gang members, who I'd earlier convinced I was not Jake Zane.

They take a position three wide, filling the boardwalk so no one can pass.

And, foolishly, both my Colt and my pocket pistol are in my sailcloth cabin aboard the *Windsong*.

## 9

My pa wasn't the only one full of advice. My ma told me never act hastily and always evaluate the situation…but there are times others won't give you time to take time to evaluate. This seems one of those times. My ma is a word person, and insisted we learn a new one every day and one of the luxuries we carried on the wagon west was a fat dictionary.

I remember the biggest of the three Wallabys had been called Ian by one of the others the last time we crossed paths. He gives me a wicked missing-tooth smile as he palms a revolver.

"Zane, by God if that ain't a fancy straw lid. Hope it's my size. I done think you told us a black lie last time we run into each other."

I clear my throat, still trying to evaluate. "I come from a Christian house, and we were taught never to lie."

"I don't believe you learn so well, mate. Spread that coat so I see how you're heeled."

I open my coat wide, showing I have nothing on my hip. "Naked as a newborn. I believe your sidekick there called you Ian the last time we met. So, Ian, I didn't lie, I ain't Jack Zane."

My evaluation is working fine, as I see a nicely dressed plainsman—looks to be wearing a badger fur hat, clean buckskins, with a fancy beaded off-white shirt of what I'd guess is elk skin, and knee-high moccasins. He approaches behind the three, and he's well-heeled with revolvers on both sides, left and right. The one on his right hip is facing butt forward, so, evaluating, I conclude he's left-handed.

The beer-keg shaped Wallaby guffaws and blubbers, "Hell, Ian, he ain't even armed. Let's just cut the damn fool up. He deserves to die slow what he did to our mates."

Ian holsters his revolver and draws that ivory-handled pigsticker they all wear. "I believe I'll filet you like a flounder."

The oncoming plainsman, appearing twice my age with a demeanor and body speaking of years in the sun and weather, eating what he picked wild, caught, or killed, pushes between the three of them in a brazen manner befitting a man with a firearm on each hip. I'm six feet from Ian, who's still smiling and showing that missing tooth. In two strides the plainsman is passing and is a step beyond before he realizes I've pulled the Colt off his right hip, and by the time he turns it's blowing fire and smoke.

Ian hits the boardwalk flat on his back, screaming and then doubled up, with both hands grasping the knee I've shot a big bloody chunk out of. The other two are trying to shove their knives back into the sheaths as it's suddenly a gun fight and at the same time pull their revolvers.

But my borrowed one is again cocked and panning

back and forth from one Wallaby's gut to the other. "Who's next?" I ask.

Both of them slowly lift their hands away from their revolvers.

I snap at the short, fat one. "Two finger Mr. Ian's pistol, please. Then drop it and kick it over my way right after both of you drop your gun belts on the boardwalk. Don't make me nervous…my trigger finger's a twitch already."

I glance over at the plainsman, who seems more amused than angered by my borrowing without taking time to ask. I say, over my shoulder not taking my eyes off the three, "I owe you for powder, cap, and ball, sir. If you'll oblige me another minute or so, I'll settle up."

Ian is screaming so loud I can barely hear myself, so I admonish him, "Mr. Ian, stop that caterwauling or I'll be forced to take a chunk out of the other knee."

He goes silent as a church mouse. Then mumbles to his mates, his teeth chattering among rugged breaths, "Get me a doc. And bloody fast."

"Back away from those belts," I growl at the two, and they do, with hands extended as if they can block the shots they expect me to fire. "Now, drop the knives alongside the belts. Then pick this pile of crap up and haul him to the sawbones, leaving your accoutrements where they lay."

The plainsman chuckles as they drag Ian to his feet and loop an arm over each of their shoulders, and stumble away.

"I guess you got yourself three firearms now, young man. So how about returning mine."

I ease the hammer then flip it and catch the barrel and hand it butt first. Then I gather up the two gun belts, the loose revolver, and the three pigstickers, stuff them inside, then sling my satchel of newly acquired weapons and store-bought goods over my shoulder. I turn back and extend my hand. "I owe you, sir. I'm Jake Zane."

He shakes. "Obadiah Barnabas. Friends call me Obey. And fast as you are with the smoke cannon, I believe I'd like to keep you as friend."

"My pleasure. Would you be hungry, Mr. Barnabas—"

"Obey, young man."

"Then, hungry, Obey?"

"I could sure enough eat."

"I'm scheduled for lunch at the Niantic, and I'd be obliged if you'd join us."

"Way above the contents of my purse, Jake."

"My treat, sir. Had you not boldly pushed your way through those brigands, I'd likely be crow bait. Or I guess seagull bait, considering the hereabouts."

"Then, sir, don't mind if I do."

As we head up the street, I'm met by two coppers, one of whom is carrying a double-barrel Coach gun. He makes his intentions known well before we grow even. "Keep your hands clear of those weapons, gentlemen." Then he eyes me up and down. "You're the one discharged his weapon on a city street."

"I'm the one kept myself from being chunked into chowder by three Sydney Ducks intent on doing me harm."

"Tell it to the judge," he says and moves closer.

"I'm due for lunch with Lord Stanley-Smyth and his guest, who I'm sure you know, Marshal Robert G. Crozier."

"Bull crap," the copper says.

"The Niantic is only another block. How about you fellas let us lead the way and you can verify my claims."

"Bull crap," the same copper says, but the other one cautions him.

"Mort, I think we'd better make sure he ain't lying. Crozier's got himself a temper."

They follow us, me looking like a weapons merchant with three revolvers and three knives damn near the size of dragoon French swords, in addition to my cotton sack full of store boughts.

The same doorman steps in front of our entourage, but I remember his name. "Henry, I'm Jake Zane, Lord Stanley-Smyth's employee, and we have an appointment."

In moments, at the Lord's table, both coppers have hats in hand and are apologizing for detaining us.

I'm quick to defend them. "These gentlemen are to be commended, Mr. Crozier. They were only doing their job."

The two coppers back out of the restaurant, nodding.

The Lord extends his hand and shakes then asks, "And who's your friend."

"Mr. Obadiah Barnabas, came to my aid and I owe him at least a lunch, sir."

"Then he's our guest as well. Now, tell me about your seagoing experiences."

I eat slowly and twice what I normally would, as I relate the experience of the voyage and then as Obadiah regales us with stories of the revolution. It seems he acted as a guide for the explorer Freemont who was caught up in the Mexican War. It is a propitious lunch for my new friend Obadiah, as the Lord has acquired a freight company during the days I was gone, and my new friend finds himself a well-paid shotgun guard on a six-up pulled stage.

And I find myself on my way back to the *Windsong*,

but with my bonus of one hundred six dollars in my pocket. Which means, if I conjure correctly, that one load of timber and cut lumber fetched five thousand three hundred dollars.

And should I stay for the full five and a half voyages, I'll damn near double my poke.

If I live through that many trips and don't end up in Davy Jones's locker.

## 10

I'm just settling into my bunk when First Mate McGillicutty steps through the canvas.

"Mumu has gone missing. You'll take his watch."

"Missing?"

"Didn't return from ashore. Get to it."

That worries me. "He's not the type to shirk."

"You're not his mama, get up and get with it."

I'm already pulling on my trousers, but McGillicutty loses no opportunity to chide me.

Still, I'm compelled to speak. "Maybe he's in trouble. I'd like to go ashore and find him."

"Look, Jack Nastyface, you'll do as you're told and do it now."

"Yes, sir."

"The weather is freshening so we'll bend the top sails for our passage through the narrows. We'll be as close to the wind as possible. You'll stay aloft until we turn nor'west and drop topsail, when hailed. Understand?"

"Yes, sir." This means hours perched on a topgallant yard, nearly as high as one can ascend aboard the *Wind-*

*song*. As McGillicutty stomps away, I pull off my trousers and pull on my newly acquired wool long johns, new knit hat, and wool socks, and a pair of canvas slippers Mumu has sewn for me. Brogans won't do to keep one's footing in the rigging, and a slip means a short sixty-or-more-foot descent to the hard deck, or if lucky should the ship be heeling enough, into the briny bone-chilling cold of the sea. Of course, should that be the fortunate result, then one will bob about praying the jolly boat is launched to retrieve you before a shark finds you interesting. To do without the canvas slippers means the cold may mean you lose feeling in bare feet and descending without knowing where your feet alight...well, you might as well dive.

The topgallants have been furled while at the dock, so our work won't begin until we're through the narrows, even though we have to be in position as if an emergency means drop sail, we're in position to do so.

We cast off and Cap'n Polkinghorn masterfully weaves through the abandoned ships, brigs, schooners, and barks, snapping orders with almost every breath. As we see the bank of fog occluding the narrows leading to open water, Sour John, Boston Bob, Rufus Goatherd, and I begin our foremast ascent to the topgallant. I find I'm gaining confidence in the rigging and am already seldom outclimbed. And am not this time. Of course, winning the race means you're the man farthest out on the yard away from the mast. Maybe that's why I'm first. I have to laugh wondering if ego and winning is really winning at all. Maybe these other old salts are smart enough to lose.

Even being summertime, it turns cold as soon as we enter the fogbank, and I'm glad I've wrapped myself in wool.

I'm surprised when we clear the narrows how much

the wind has freshened. If you can call a Force Five wind, I'd judge thirty knots, a "freshening." It's blowing like hell, and I see the others lash themselves to the boom, so follow suit. Should the wind increase even a little it'll be considered a gale. When the blowing fog and mist clears enough to see the surface, I'd guess the swell six or more feet and whitecaps punctuate every top.

We had one night of weather such as this on my first trip, but I was not high above the deck during that squall.

I'm sure we won't get hailed to drop sail, and am hoping we'll get the order to descend, but it doesn't come. Boston Bob is nearest me and nearer the mast, with Sour John and Rufus on the windward side of the mast. So I yell at him, "We stuck here?"

"Aye, mate. 'oly Christ, she's a bloody 'owler of a blow, over the waves we'll damn sure go."

Rather than show my wide eyes and squeak a reply, I clear my throat and ask, having to yell to make myself heard, "You don't sound the limeys I've heard, Bob. Where were you sired?"

Boston Bob laughs at that, and for a change doesn't rhyme. "Aye, mate, I was born within the sound of Bow bells."

"I don't understand?"

"Queen Vic is mine to love and respect. I'm a Brit to the marrow, mate. It means born close to the St. Mary-le-Bow church in Cheapside, London. Cockney bred and born and proud to be, and I'll trample the 'oly tar from the man speaks badly of queen and country."

"No insult here, mate," I yell back. "You gotta admire folks who conquered half the world." Then I smile and can't help but add, "Of course not us, but half the world." Then I settle back, leaning into my lashing, shutting my eyes as even the mist is cutting.

To Bob's credit he laughs and adds, "Aye, you'd be fittin' in, lubber. I'm gobsmacked that it's so."

That awakens me from my closed-eye, strained relaxation. "Gobsmacked?"

"Aye, you'd be not so good with the King's English?" he manages a shrug, still grasping the boom with both arms wrapped tightly.

"If you say so," I yell, "But what would gobsmacked mean?"

"I guess the Yank would say surprised."

I laugh, even with the hard wind in my face. "Well, I'd not be gobsmacked, my Cockney friend, as I'll fit in, eventually."

Bob laughs and makes a move to give me a little salute, then has to grab on even with being lashed tightly.

After what seems a day but is probably a couple of hours, the wind, thank God, has lessened to maybe twenty knots, and we're hailed to drop sail, and do so, and the topsails snap full with a crack resembling the discharge of a cannon. I have to slap my hands repeatedly against my thighs before I dare loosen the bowline I've tied in my lashing, but do so and follow, descending the "ladder" which is lines tied between the tar-covered stays. As I still have feeling in my feet, it reminds me to think of, and worry about, my friend Mumu. His canvas slippers likely save my life. His friendship is dear to me, and I hope the Devil has not found him with the variety of mischief common to the streets of San Francisco.

The ladder is very narrow where it lands on the mast near the boom but widens as it nears the deck. As eager as you are to find the relative safety of the deck, you have to be careful not to step on the hand of the man below, a cardinal sin. But we alight safely and Polkinghorn, with an unusual gesture, strides over.

"Smartly done, gentlemen. Retire to the galley for a bit of warmth and a bowl. Don't tarry as I'll soon enough call all hands. We'll take advantage of this blow, but if she freshens again, it'll be reef sail."

It's likely more words than we've heard from the captain during the last voyage or the beginning of this one. He's strangely loquacious this day.

Su Lee, the cook, gives me a missive as I'm sopping up my molasses, telling me to report to the Cap'n's quarters when finished.

I presume the Cap'n is sorry about the compliment he paid me, us, and is now ready to keelhaul me or at least chew me up and down about something.

## 11

I knock, am bade enter, and for a change invited to sit. I do, and inquire, as he's reading, "Sir?"

He looks up and sets his document aside. "That was roundly done up in the shrouds, young Zane. Have you spent any time in the texts I've loaned you?"

I'm sure my sigh can be heard topside. It appears I'm still in the cap'n's good graces. "Every spare moment, sir."

"So, you know a deadeye from a standing block from a triple fiddle block?"

I can't help but smile. "I know a standing block is a running block, usually for loading and off-loading. A deadeye is a pair of fixed blocks to tighten stays. Triple fiddle? Sorry, no idea, sir."

"Much like a running block, but with three lines rather than two."

"Thank you. I'll learn."

"And you have, young Jake, much faster than most. I received a letter from Lord Stanley-Smyth just before we cast off. He'd like you to transfer to the *Orient* upon our return from this run."

I'm a little taken aback, then ask, "So, the *Orient* is a full tri-masted square-rigged ship?"

"She is. She's in port now having repairs done, then off to the Sandwich Islands again."

"May I speak freely?"

"As I've mentioned before, I'll take any comment so long as it's respectful."

I clear my throat. "First, I feel an obligation to find my friend Mumu and make sure he is faring well, which I plan to do with every free minute upon our return. Second, I've yet to learn this ship and know it'll take a year or more to do so. Unless I make my escape when the promised five and a half voyages are complete, I'm far from leaving Jack Nastyman behind and becoming part of the family I've learned a happy crew becomes. And, not to seem the sycophant, I admire your leadership and knowledge. So, I'd as soon stay aboard."

"I'd be a liar if I didn't say I'm pleased." Then he quickly adds, "Pleased, but don't take that as an endorsement. You still should have signed on as a common seaman and you're still fathoms from a real second mate."

I nod with a compliant, "Yes, sir."

He continues, "I suggest you take the time, out of hunting for Mr. Mumu upon our return, to inform Stanley-Smyth of your desire to stay with the *Windsong*. You may tell him I comply with your wishes."

"Yes, sir."

"So be it, back to Mr. McGillicutty to find your duty. Use my ladder."

I hesitate on the first rung of his ladder to the wheelhouse. "Sir, if I may?"

"Go ahead."

"Do you think we'll ever get as far as the Columbia?"

"I don't normally confide ship's plans to the crew, but should we not find a load before, we'll head for Elliott Bay, well past the Columbia. Rumor is they're cutting both red cedar and Sitka spruce, as well as some Douglas fir."

"Thank you, sir," I say, and continue up. That brings a smile to my sunburned face as I still have the intent of finding my first and only love—not that I'm sure what love is—who is supposedly with her family in the Willamette Valley, near the mouth of the great Columbia River. She, and that stolen kiss on the Oregon Trail, still fill my dreams the nights when I'm not too exhausted to dream.

---

WHEN ONLY THREE DAYS OUT, in rough weather, we drop anchor off what is called a doghole port—any tough anchorage without a barrier to the open sea is so called. But there is sign of a mill and timber being harvested. A partially clear-cut mountainside means a mill nearby. Polkinghorn wants no other lumber ships to beat him to the bounty. He'd heard of its establishment, so turned east at the proper latitude, and as an example of his skill, soon sighted the clear-cuts through his ship's telescope. Sailor's Shroud Point does not have the most admirable name—in fact a fearful one—but we drop anchor and McGillicutty, with two sailors to man the oars of a jolly boat, Jack Pyle and Boston Bob, rides to the beginning of the breakers then rides the waves ashore. I'd quickly learned it is nearly impossible to judge the surf from the ocean side, and we'd misjudged this one we quickly learned, as the jolly boat disappears from sight more than once in the valleys of high swells trying to make landfall.

With the soundings taken we 'd been forced to drop anchor nearly three hundred yards offshore. So far it is impossible to hear a man's shouts, particularly over a breaking surf. But McGillicutty and Polkinghorn have their own sign language.

We quickly learn that the first mate has hand signaled the harvest is spoken for, and worse, he will not be able to broach the surf to return to the ship. The cap'n quickly concludes that the barometer is falling fast, and the storm isn't likely to let up for days. He signs to the first mate that we'll try and pick him up on the return.

So, we sail on, our nose as close to the wind as possible, heading west'nor'west so we don't have to beat directly against the current. By the time we reach Humboldt's latitude, we are in a full Force Six gale, and nearing shore is a fool's errand, so the cap'n continues northerly. I had secret hopes it would be Elliott Bay, and before that the Columbia River, before the storm recedes, but soon change my tune as we are now three crew short and with the storm the work is nearly continuous and meals almost impossible to cook aboard a ship heeling forty-five degrees. I am about to decide no matter the money that sea life is not for this sod breaker, when the wind quiets to a mere fifteen knots and shifts off the port quarter with us on a due north course. A course that will bring us again near terra firma only a hundred and seventy miles south of Elliott Bay, and very near the mouth of the Columbia.

Am I to see the lady who makes my heart race?

———

IN A DAY my hopes are dashed when Polkinghorn again turns due east then back north to track the coast and search for signs of a lumber camp, and as luck would have it—the ship's good luck and my bad—soon sights signs of a clear-cut on a steep mountain shoreline. This time it's an easy trip for the remaining jolly boat, with the captain in the bow and Baldy Olafsson and young Taggart on the oars.

They almost as quickly return with news that this camp has a barge of forty by sixty feet, already more than half loaded with timbers. I know the captain prefers cut lumber, but it can be milled near San Francisco, so we find he's made a bargain and the barge, towed by two twenty-five-foot longboats, will be alongside and our next day will be spent taking on spruce and Douglas fir.

No Willamette for me. No young lady. At least not this trip.

## 12

With a full load there's little reason to stress rigging on the run home, so we are able to lay off Sailor's Shroud Point until the tide quiets and McGillicutty, Boston Bob, and the Caribbean Jack Pyle are back aboard. And we give thanks for the fact as the workload is now back to normal.

With the exception of sailing a few knots in the midst of a pod of gray whales, who seem as interested in us as we are in them, we have an uneventful sail back to San Francisco, with timbers stacked eight feet deep on the decks. Watching these giant creatures broach and blow makes one wonder about his place among living things, we humans are puny creatures compared to many who have a place on God's good earth.

The few small docks are full, so we have to moor two hundred yards from terra firma and tie up alongside an abandoned ship of equal length. The *Central America* is stripped of masts and booms, her deckhouses torn down, even a good part of her decks removed and one can see below into cabins and holds. Not a stick of furniture or benches remain and even the iron cookstove is gone...probably boiling beans in some city hash house. But she must be anchored soundly as she's been in the same spot for nearly a year, or so says McGillicutty.

Cap'n Polkinghorn takes pity on me and my wish to make sure Mumu is alright and has not been shanghaied by another vessel, so I'm on the first trip of our jolly boat ashore even before we've off-loaded our cargo, which we can't do until dock space is available. Jack Pyle has offered to help me in my quest. It seems Jack, being a man of color also, had also been a close friend of Mumu's, and is as concerned as myself. We alight in the jolly at nine in the morning, given twenty-four hours before we're expected back aboard. He does allow me to retrieve my scattergun and one of my Colts before I depart.

My big surprise is alighting on the dock from the jolly boat to be met by Jack Pyle, who came in the load ahead of me. He has a flyer in hand.

"This was posted on the light pole, Jake. This ain't good." He hands it to me.

It's a poor likeness of me, which bothers me less than the printing: Wanted Sailor Jake Zane, for the wonton shooting of our fellow Australian Ian Burnie. Loss of a leg. Reward $500, Five Hundred Dollars. Payable in gold coin with the delivery of Zane or his head to Wallaby Club Headquarters.

I give a little chuckle, but I'm not really amused.

Pyle adds, "The coppers was pulling them down, saying it was not legal, so that's some relief."

"Some," I say, "but how many have been seen? The scum on these streets would kill for a five-dollar gold piece, much less five hundred."

"Maybe you should lay this leave over a'board the *Windsong*?"

"I got business hereabout."

"Then step careful," Jack says, and looks sincerely concerned.

The streets are relatively quiet as we walk up away from the waterfront, the Barbary Coast as it's called. The only folks I know are Lord Stanley-Smyth, who doesn't hobnob with the common folk, and, it dawns on me, I've met and could call on San Francisco's number one copper, Marshal Robert G. Crozier. Seems his employees are doing the right thing, tearing down the flyers. Of course, what I've learned of San Francisco coppers, it may be one of them tries to collect and they may be tearing down the flyers so they have no competition collecting on my head.

With Jack trailing closely, I head for the Niantic Hotel, and am pleased to see Henry's top hat standing tall out of the growing crowd. He's opening the door to a hack as we stride up, and I have to wait for him to trek inside with a load of fancy leather luggage, a beautiful lady behind, and a foppish fellow who sports a walking stick with a gold duck for a handpiece, a pin-striped suit of clothes, and a waistcoat as pink as a cherry blossom trailing both.

"When you have a moment," I say to Henry as he passes with two leather valises and a hatbox under one arm.

The fop seems to take offense at my inquiry. "Stand aside, blackguard," he snaps.

I ignore him, as much as I have the inclination to shove his walking stick where the sun don't shine.

Jack and I wait patiently for his return. Henry gives

me a chuckle and asks, "What's your pleasure, young blackguard?"

"I admire your patience and restraint, Henry. I don't guess Lord Stanley-Smyth is about?"

"He and his Lady were off to Sacramento on the new steamship three days ago, due back this evening. They have a supper affair scheduled and some string quartet playing, likely until midnight. What's this about the Wallabys wanting your head?"

"Wanting and getting are two different things."

"Aye, but I'd be careful. They're a shiftless lot, but dangerous. Tread careful."

"Thanks for your concern. I will." Then I change the subject. "It really isn't the Lord I'm hunting. We have a friend you might have seen. He didn't make the ship a little over a week ago when we sailed. Mumu he's called, a head taller than me, more'n twice my weight, but the most distinguishing feature is he's tattooed full face, arms, and hands. A Sandwich Islander. Dark skin, lots of coal-black hair."

"Hummmm," Henry says, his chin resting on a fist. "Don't know any of those fellas by name, and a few of them are about. I do know they seem to gather over around the barracoons, on Stockton Street, a couple of blocks up above Buena Vista Cove."

"Thank you, Henry. I'll stand you to a mug or two when we're bar leaning in a saloon."

"And I'll happily partake with you, sir."

I spin on my heel, but he stops me with a warning. "That's a rough spot you're headed for, young Mr. Zane. I see you're well-heeled, but even then, those barbarians will shoot you down for a penny for your purse and steal your boots as well."

"I appreciate the warning. I did forget to ask, where would the marshal's office be?"

"Only three blocks from the barracoons, in the City Hall at Pacific and Montgomery. Watch your back," then he laughs. "Watch not only the brigands around the barracoons, but the politicians around city hall. Fact is, I don't know which gaggle of louts is worse."

We both laugh as I stride off with Jack close behind. Not wanting to appear the bumpkin, I didn't ask Henry but rather now ask Jack, "What would a barracoon be?"

"Why, Mr. Zane, it be a brothel full of loose ladies, but more, a place where you can buy a Chinese girl, if you have the silver. Every second Tuesday there be an auction and girls are sold to the highest bidder."

"You mean for a poke, for an hour, or for the night?" I ask.

"No, sir. Just like the slave markets in New Orleans. You buys one, she be yours to work, to breed, or whatsomever."

I'm silent for a minute as we stride back toward the waterfront, then have to exclaim, "Hell, Jack, this ain't a slave state."

"Tell them poor Chinee girls that. And them ol' fat boys what buy 'em. I seen two shiploads of Chinee girls, some young as the first cherry blossom in spring and pretty as a lotus bloom, and they herd 'em right into them barracoons. I hear'd tell some bring a thousand or more. One gritty ol' miner fresh off the mountain throwed down a nugget said to weigh a pound for one."

"Don't the coppers have anything to say?"

He guffaws. "Hell, them coppers come around once't a week and they line them palms with more'n I make in a year, or so the scuttlebutt say."

"That ain't right," I have to mumble.

"Right don't seem to count if there be a pile of coin or dust at stake."

The plank streets are beginning to bustle as hacks, beer wagons, handcarts, horsebackers, hacks, and buggies rattle by. I'd been told that the city has changed drastically over the past year, blossomed with formerly scarce goods. Where it was once difficult to find a potato, now loaded carts of all kinds of fresh vegetables filled city handcarts and markets. Potatoes are no longer a rarity; turnips can be had at a moderate price at least compared to a year ago. The markets make pleasant morning sights and fragrances. Besides vegetables and fruits, fish and game of all descriptions from the ocean, the bay, the interior valley, and distant Sierras fill markets and carts. Slabs of smoked salmon, vast quantities of flounder, crab, petrale, whole cartloads of geese, ducks, quail, and sandhill crane, quarters of bear, elk, antelope and deer hang, and smaller game load the stalls of dealers and cast their fragrance over the neighborhood. Mutton is rare as the Catholic missions are an ocean of beef, and excellent beef is in abundance.

We wander west, dodging wagons dumping sand into the sea, pushing the waterfront out and creating new lots, and soon come to Buena Vista Cove, then start up the hill on Pacific. I thought the harbor front, the Barbary Coast, rough, but quickly decide it's a wander through a shaded glen compared to this couple of blocks. More and more layabouts line the street, most smoking or chewing and spitting on the boardwalk. There's not a woman in sight, but then I glance up and women line the second-story windows, perched like colorful birds, but missing a few feathers as I see enough skin to make me blush outright. I'm staring at a particularly pretty one and run smack into a light post, dang near give myself a bloody nose. Half the street break out in laughter, and even Jack chuckles.

"Probably outta watch the boardwalk," he says when he quits chuckling. "Dang if they ain't pickpockets and highbinders on every corner."

I cough and agree. "I'll pay attention."

By the time we reach the third cross street, I pull up short. "That looks like Mumu."

"You be right, and them is hand-and-leg irons them two coppers have on him."

## 13

Mumu is bleeding from nose, cut lip, and a gash on his forehead, red blood decorating his already tattoo-decorated face, dripping off his chin. One of the five coppers has an arm hanging loose and his face is puckered as if he's about to bawl. Two others bleed from a variety of knots on head and cheekbones. One copper has an arm over the shoulders of another, his head hangs as if he's barely conscious.

Mumu sees us coming and yells, "Mr. Zane, Mr. Zane, it be my sister. De' got her in dis place."

I nod and approach, but am warned by a copper, who shakes his nightstick at me. "Stand back. Don't interfere."

"No, sir. I have no intent to interfere in the work of the police. However, that's my friend—"

"No matter. He's off to jail and if you don't move back, you'll be joining him."

I take two steps back. "May I ask what he's done?"

"Took all of us to take him down. The som'bitch is a bull."

"Yes, sir. That I know, but what's he done?"

"He was told to leave the premises and refused."

"This is a brothel, right. He says his sister—"

"Stand aside," he again shakes his nightstick at me. Then adds, "And don't touch them weapons."

Hard not to touch the Coach gun I carry, but I keep the muzzle pointed straight at the boardwalk.

An ominous, black-lacquered wagon reins up, pulled by a pair of handsome blacks with a bright, brass-trimmed harness, two brass lanterns, and brass fittings on its wheels. It would easily hold eight lawbreakers, with a door in the back with a tiny, barred window. The copper who's been warning me off steps over and opens the door. Three others drag Mumu that way, but the big man slams two of them together, kicks the third one in his personals who turns green and goes to his knees, and Mumu, even though another copper has leaped on his back and encircled his neck with a blue-uniformed arm, begins to lope away.

"Halt!" yells the one with the nightstick, but he drops it and tries to fumble a revolver from a flapped holster.

He gets it lifted and sighted in, but his fellow copper is hanging on Mumu's back as he now canters away, and firing would mean he'd have to shoot through his associate to hit his target. When a half block away, Mumu reaches back over his shoulder, has the man on his back by the collar, and flings him aside onto a cart chuck-full of fish.

Fish, merchant, upended cart, and copper scatter about the boardwalk as Mumu disappears among the road traffic.

Studying the copper with the pistol still raised, I almost believe he's happy to see Mumu disappear from his life. He sighs deeply, then turns to me.

"You know that man. You're coming to the station with me."

I shrug. "I can't help you, sir. I know him casually from the street," I lie.

"I'll have the scattergun." He gathers it up, and fishes my Colt out of its holster. "You're coming, in chains or willingly, your choice."

"As you wish, sir," I say. I turn to Jack who's been silent through all this, and wave him away, and he fades into the growing spectators.

The copper who had been assisted by others has been dropped and is face-first on the boardwalk. Two others again lift him and support him, the one who'd played the remora on Mumu's back staggers up, seemingly none the worse for his journey other than smelling of fish. And we're away, the stick-wielder leading, the fish-smelling copper following, me sandwiched between, and three, attached like Siamese triplets, following. The supported one still dragging his feet in a stupor.

It seems I found my friend, and happily lost him again. Now, to talk myself out of the clutches of five wounded, angry, and likely, embarrassed, coppers.

Luckily as they escort me into City Hall and to Police Headquarters, Marshal Crozier is walking out. Of course, he doesn't recognize me.

"Marshal Crozier," I call to him.

He glances at me, then totally ignores me, and continues on.

"Shut your piehole," the copper leading the way, snaps over his shoulder.

"Marshal, it's Jake Zane, Lord Stanley-Smyth's employee."

The copper with the nightstick spins on his heel and

raises the stick. I cover my head with both arms, preferring a broken arm to a broken head.

"Hold on, Smithers!" the marshal yells.

After a few minutes explaining why I was hauled in, Crozier instructs the copper he'd called Smithers, "Sergeant, take a written statement from young Zane and send him on his way. He's Lord Stanley-Smyth's man, easily found again."

"Yes, sir," Smithers says, then turns to me. "You can write, right?"

"Yes, sir, given quill and ink." I write a cursory statement.

I can see Smithers and his copper mates are not happy with the marshal's instruction, but keep their lips buttoned. I rise to leave, giving Smithers a perfunctory salute.

"Thank you, Sergeant, for not lollygagging me with that shillelagh."

"The day is young, and I still have high hopes," he says with a slight curl of his lip.

"My firearms, please?"

And he returns them, but I can see it pains him to do so.

"Have a nice day," I say, spinning on my heel and heading out the door. Across the plank street, leaning on a light pole, Jack Pyle waits. He'd found a tobacco cart and filled his pipe, and smoke curls from his lips. I hurry over.

"I see no knots on your noggin," he says with a smile.

"Thank the good Lord and my luck in having influential friends."

"Aye, and now back to the ship and out of harm's way?"

"No, back to the hunt for friend Mumu, and then to hide him on the ship."

"And a dogged old sea dog ye be. He may be even harder to find, now that he knows every lubber with a stick and badge is on the hunt for him."

"If his sister is truly in that brothel, and particularly if against her will, Mumu won't be far. He'll be like a big shark waiting to pounce on prey."

Jack glances up at the sun, disappearing over the buildings to the west. "I'd guess we have some eighteen or so hours to find the sogger, so maybe we should split up?"

"Not a bad idea. Don't you get waylaid. I don't want to be hunting you both."

"Keep a sharp eye, mate. You attract trouble like a wounded sardine to a seal."

"That saloon right at the foot of the dock?"

"Murphy's?"

"I'll meet you back there at sundown."

"Done," Jack says, and strides away, uphill, leaving me the downhill direction, which is fine as that's the way Mumu headed.

Now, to find him before a half-dozen coppers, which it would take, make a mush melon out of his head.

## 14

I'VE ONLY GONE A HALF BLOCK BEFORE I RUN INTO SOUR John, Tag Taggart, and Boston Bob stumbling out of a saloon. I quickly fill them in on the happenings and Mumu's peril, and they, too, are on the hunt. Our odds of finding our shipmate more than double.

I walk the waterfront all the way to the north side of Buena Vista Bay, then reverse, asking storekeepers, cart vendors, and seafarers who seem to be merely lounging and enjoying a smoke, if they've seen my very easily identified friend. I stroll and question all the way west and south to Mission Bay. As it's getting dark, I double-time it back to Murphy's Saloon, which turns out to be Murphy's Saloon and Seafood, with a pot large enough for several hundred crabs near the batwing entry doors. A Black man tends the crab pot, regularly dropping live ones in the east side and fishing out cooked ones with a large paddle on the west. They smell far worse than they taste, I've learned. He piles them on a tray which is snatched up by a rosy-cheeked, chubby lass wearing a gathered orchid-colored blouse, but gathered low enough that a crevice large enough to accommodate one of my Colts is the gap between freckled breasts.

She's ferrying platters of crab into the crowded establishment and has returned for a refill twice as I approach. I push through the batwings and let my eyes adjust to the dim, and smoky light. Two dealers are hard at work with tables full of faro players. All four of my shipmates lean against the bar, foaming mugs of beer in front, and foam-covered mustaches expose their pastime.

"Any luck?" I ask, as Sour John orders me a mug. It's a beverage I've yet to acquire a taste for, but I guess now is as good a time as any.

Boston Bob answers, with a smile but a worried one. "Good luck, and bad. Found him in de bushes near de Presidio. But 'e refuses to join us until 'e's sprung 'is sister from that barracoon joint."

"Does he need help?" I ask.

"Dat barracoon place is fulla Chinee fellows with hatchets, and 'e'll need all de 'elp he can muster up. And 'e say they be a dozen or more girls up in the attic, wait'n to be auctioned off. His sister was stole from his mama and papa down in Monterey, and hauled up here. I guess she's a large lass but a mite prettier than Mumu." That gets a laugh, but I turn them serious.

"So, that's me lendin' a hand. How about you fellows."

Sour John joins the conversation. "You got that scattergun and sidearm. We got nothing but marlinspikes and folding knives. Don't seem much against hatchets."

I contemplate that for a moment. I can't return to the ship for the rest of my weapons but have an idea. "I passed a wheelwright a block or so back. A two-foot hardwood spoke will serve you well…particularly with me backing y'all up with this Coach gun. You can draw straws for the loan of the Colt."

They look at each other, then back at me and all nod.

I glance around and find a discarded chopstick in the gutter and break it into four pieces, one noticeably shorter than the others, turn my back to my mates and arrange them in my hand so the length doesn't show, and turn back.

"Who draws first?" I ask. And Sour John steps forward and pulls the short one right off.

"That's it," I say, and hand the Colt over as the others grumble. I can't help but ask, "John, can you shoot with only one eye?"

He gives me a sardonic glare. "Close one and see if you can."

He's right, I only aim with one eye. "Sorry, just asking." I change the subject. "Let's find Mumu again and lay out a plan. He stands out like a whale in a school of mackerel, so I guess it's nighttime before we try anything."

The others grumble about Sour John drawing the Colt without them having a chance, but that's the luck of the draw and I ignore them.

And Boston Bob reminds me. "Him standing out ain't our only worry. Hooligans see that flyer then you and we gotta scurry."

"Bob," I have to comment, "should you not think of a rhyme, you just don't say what's on your mind, or what?"

"Can't rhyme, it ain't worth a dime," he says, and laughs.

I just shake my head.

So we head for the wheelwright. We're six strong, when we tie up with Mumu, but I have my scattergun and Sour John my Colt, so I am robbed of three dollars at six bits per for near two-foot-long hardwood spokes. They are fancy turned and have a flare at the axel end, which makes for a fine club. I wouldn't want to have one across my pate.

We find Mumu in a copse of trees near the Presidio Fort and gather up out of sight of the road to form our plan.

It seems Terrill 'Tag' Taggart, who's my age, to my surprise has visited the brothel part of the barracoon many times, and knows the layout of the building well, so he takes the stage. He's backed up by Sour John, who's also taken a turn at the ladies of the night there.

Tag begins. "The bottom floor is a saloon and gambling hall, doors leading out back, one private, one to the privies. Two stairways lead up, one on each side of the room, the bar is across three-quarters of the back wall. The privy door on the south or left side as you enter. The privies are in a small yard, only seven or eight feet wide, with a six-foot fence twixt them and whatever's across. Up each stairway, and I've been up both," he gives us a sheepish smile, "is a hall the length of the building, maybe fifty feet, with cribs on both sides and a window at the end. When out at the privy I noticed ladders aside each window, all the way to the third floor. From the hallway on the south side there be another small stairway climbing up to another door, but it's enclosed in a lathe cage with a locked door. Marked with a big private sign. Says **PRIVATE, KEEP OUT, ENTER AND BE SHOT DEAD**. The door above hosts the same sign.

He seems finished so I turn to Sour John. "Anything to add?"

"Nope, 'ceptin' the cribs is about ten by ten and each one has a lumpy bed, a pitcher and bowl and bar of lye soap on a sideboard, and some have windows, but high and tiny. Seems them Tong boys don't want them girls climbing out and on the run."

I nod. "Since you mentioned it, them Tong boys? Guards?"

John continues. "One by the batwings, one sitting shotgun on the north wall. One moving free and easy through the crowd. Whenever I was there the only white man was a big Irish bloke tending bar. He speaks that Chinee jabber like he was born there. There's a small bandstand but I understand there ain't never no music, only a place for the auctioneer and to display the flesh when they sell them girls. Probably more of them Tong fellas beyond the private door, and likely up on the third floor, where I 'spose they keep the sales goods."

"Arms?" I ask.

"Shotgun guard has a Coach gun, a'course, and the others have one of them short hatchets in their sash. I'd guess the Irishman has a scattergun in easy reach."

I rub my chin in thought. "So, likely, unless they put her to work, Mumu's sister is upstairs on the third floor." I turn to Mumu, who's been silent through this whole conversation.

"You agree, Mumu?"

He ignores the question. "You fellas my shipmates, not my war mates. I do this meself."

"No, sir," I interrupt. "We're your mates, and we're in this hell or high water."

He lowers his big head and I think for a moment he's going to break into tears.

Then he lifts his head, and in a strong voice proclaims, "I not forget my mates, never, ever, do I forget." He looks from man to man and nods at each. "We free all girls, not just sister. She not go easy to crib so probably upstairs being beaten until she go quiet. But she die first."

I give him a nod, and add, "Then we take the guards and bartender and herd them ahead of us up that stairway. If they don't have a key we break it down. We keep them ahead of us in case we're met by gunfire from the third floor." I turn to Sour John. "You'll stay at the head of the first stairway, making sure no Tong boys follow us up. You've got the Colt and can discourage them. Okay?"

"Sure as the sun sets in the west," John says.

"Do those guards and bartender tip a few suds while working?"

Sour John offers, "I was there early, not even dark yet, and they was all acceptin' drinks from the customers lookin' for favors and to be directed to the prettiest of the ladies."

"So, we'll give them a while to get in their cups. Are there coppers about?"

"Seems they come and go," Tag said. "Saw one drop by for a free shot of hooch one time, but he didn't linger."

"Then, we'll go when it's dead dark, presuming there's no city copper on hand. Good to go?" And I look from man to man and get a nod from each.

Now, to wait for dark.

## 15

The building doesn't have a sign, at least in English, but a spate of Chinese characters run the width of the building between the first and second doors over many-paned windows flanking a set of batwing swingers, but the like of which I'd never seen. The steps leading up to the doors are flanked by a pair of six-foot-long lounging statues that look like lions, but from my reading I know them to be Chinese dogs. The batwings appear to be solid gold. I realize the reason for a pair of two-inch-thick doors that when closed shut off access to the saloon and to what must be valuable gold-covered batwings. But not solid as when I shove one open it is as light as the normal oak-slatted ones. I guess the gold to be some kind of paint or superthin covering, but still cold to the touch as I push inside.

We've decided to go in separately so as not to be so noticeable. I'm first, Tag and Sour John follow—John with the Colt hidden beneath his twill shirt. Boston Bob will come in next. Mumu will enter only after he looks over the batwings and sees us heading for the stairway with the guards and bartender leading the way.

I'm a bit surprised to see a guard just inside, a white man with an Australian accent, who's also wielding a Coach gun. He stops me with a gruff, "No firearms or blades allowed, pilgrim. Leave 'em here."

I spread my arms wide to show I'm not carrying and give him a stupid grin. "My ma said it was dangerous to carry firearms." He waves me on in.

It appears I have a serious limp, a stiff leg, as I gimp toward the bar. I dodge past both natty-dressed men looking like bankers and merchants, and sailors and townsmen who might be hack or beer wagon whips or draymen.

Sour John and Tag are inside, their spokes stuffed into their pants at the small of their back under their coats. Had it been time for a chuckle I would have done so as they both have a ridge down their back like a humpback whale. The door guard must be as bored as the big Chinese fellow on the platform.

Limping to the bar I belly up between a couple of rough-looking louts, more in place than I would have been between bankers, and order a beer. I drop my dime on the bar and turn and place my back against it to survey the room. The shotgun guard perches on a four-foot-high platform, not much wider or deeper than the chair he occupies. Only a few feet from him is a six-foot-high by ten-foot-wide folding screen, its two-foot sections painted black with gold-and-red dragons across the bottom and beautiful gold-and-green fish across the top. I cannot see what it conceals but it must be something, not just decoration. The guard is bored. He yawns as his eyes roved over the three dozen who play faro, spin a wheel of chance, or ogle the half-dozen soiled doves who work the room.

Thankfully, there is no copper in the place. Nor have I seen one nearby outside. I place my beer on the bar and wander over to the painted Chinese screen, and step behind. It shelters a stack of brass spittoons, a pair of mops, and two buckets.

I loosen my trousers and slip the Coach gun out, check the loads, and keep it behind my leg as I limp out and over to the platform guard.

He glances at me with little interest then his attention goes to Sour John and Tag, who are putting on a bit of a show, yelling at each other as John pokes Tag in the chest with a forefinger.

"Hey, take outside!" the guard yells and stands enough that I can slip his chair six inches my way, all it needs, and as he sits back down it lurches my way and over he goes, dropping the shotgun and hitting hard with both hands extended.

I drive both barrels into the back of his neck pinning him down as Mumu crashes through the batwings and takes that guard ahead of him into and over a faro table, scattering men, table, and chairs in all directions. He comes up with the guard's Coach gun in hand.

The bartender is quick to snatch a single-shot sawed-off scattergun from under the bar but has no idea the two fellas standing across are part of our gang of rescuers. He swings it my way, but Sour John has a hand on the barrel and jerks it out of his hands. Luckily not into his own gut, but it does fire and blows a three-foot hole out of that beautiful painted screen. A half-dozen patrons make it out the batwings before Tag runs to them and pulls the heavy outside doors shut, and drops an iron bar into place, securing them.

I yell until I get silence from the crowd. "You fellas go back to your beers and whiskey. We ain't here to rob you or this horrid place. We just got a lady to find and free. So take your seats, play a little cards, drink all the free beer you want…just don't try and open those doors and leave."

The men are stirring and talking among themselves. I keep an eye on the door on the north end of the bar, marked private, expecting a dozen Tong members to charge inside carrying firearms and hatchets…but so far so good.

Tag, Sour John, and Bob each have purloined shotguns, and Tag has relieved the door guard of a revolver. So things have changed considerable.

We herd the guards ahead of us. As planned Sour John takes a position halfway up the stairway and continues to pan the room with the scattergun while we charge up the stairs behind the guards and bartender.

I guess the Tong gang members on the top floor heard the blast of the bartender's single-shot scattergun, as they are charging down as we charge up, and they've foolishly opened the doors to the third floor, and left them open.

The good news is they are a bit confused to run face-to-face into their mates, who are leading the herd, the bad is they aren't confused for long. All of them wear red sashes and top hats, as if they think they are President Millard Fillmore. The Chinaman leading the pack of three is almost as big as Mumu, and carries a hatchet in one hand and a three-foot-thick bladed executioner's sword in the other. The two behind him carry sawed-off double-barreled scatterguns. I'd guess them to be ten gauge as through the crowd of guards they look the size of six-pound cannons.

I'm the first behind the barracoon employees, who scatter against walls and three drop to the floor, while the fourth runs to the rear window to jerk it open, but it appears nailed shut.

The big man swings the sword over his head and charges me, and I have no choice. I'm centered on his wide chest with my scattergun and yell, "Stop, stop, stop!" but the third stop is unheard as Tag has cut loose with both barrels and it stops the big man in his tracks, and his forward motion is now reversed as he goes to his back and slides into the two following. Those two spin on their heels and run for the window. Not bothering to try and open it, they shove the bartender through the panes, shattering them and the mullions. They both use their hatchets to clean the remnants away and are out on the ladders and disappear.

Bob still has a charged scattergun, so I yell at him, "Watch this bunch! We're going up," and I charge up the stairs behind Mumu with Tag following.

Mumu stops, filling the doorway at the head of the stairs, and I hear him scream, then shout, "God…no, God!"

## 16

I crowd up beside Mumu to see what he's beholding with such astonishment, and see the room crowded with women, or better said young girls, all Chinese except the one standing slightly ahead of the others. She's a half-head taller than all and more than a head taller than some. She's half naked, as are all of them, her with breasts the size of muskmelons, both of which are tattooed with a flower. Her face is swollen badly and her arms and legs bruised with some new dark-blue splatches and some older brown ones.

"Malani," Mumu manages, and strides forward and throws his arms around her. The other girls back up, as if afraid of the big man.

"Do y'all have clothes?" I ask, and only one seems to understand. She steps forward. A pretty girl with cheeks reddened by some concoction, and hair tied in a bun. Her torso is wrapped with what might be a bedsheet.

"I am Yee Jaio, please call me Jaio." She turns to the others and snaps out an order, and all of them scatter to bunks lining the walls and strip away the bedsheets and are soon wrapped, looking like Roman senators. But barefoot.

Tag looks at me, a little bewildered. "What are we gonna do with more'n a dozen Chinee girls?"

"First, we're gonna get them outta this slave market." I speak to the one called Jaio. "Tell them to follow. We're going to get you ladies out of this place."

She jabbers to the others, and I lead the way, Mumu behind me, his sister's arm over his shoulder. When we reach the stairway to the saloon, Sour John yells up as soon as I'm in sight. "They're banging on the door, yelling police. I don't think we're going out the front."

"Then the back. Don't shoot any coppers. I don't want to sail on that bark they're using as a prison ship."

And we charge out the back to the small yard housing the privies. There's a six-foot plank fence and I have no idea what's beyond. I should have paid attention.

No gate. I step over and wrap Mumu's sister's arm over my shoulder. Easily done as she's almost as tall as I am, then nod at Mumu. "Make a hole," I say.

He charges the fence and planks fly away and the ladies pile after him. Tag, Sour John, and Boston Bob are covering our retreat and follow Malani, Mumu's sister, and I through the breech in the fence. Beyond is a now nearly vacant lot, with the remnants of stone walls on either side, what's left of a building burned out in last year's fire, I'd guess. It's dead dark and we have to carefully pick our way through the rubble. As soon as we reach the plank street, I yell at the others.

"I've got an idea where we can gain safety for these ladies. Hide out in the trees near the fort. It may be morning before I can get there, but God willing you'll hear me yelling."

Mumu shakes his head no. "I take Malani to Papa in Monterey."

"You have the coach fare?" I ask.

"Have twenty-dollar piece," he says.

I dig in my pocket and come up with two tens, and Sour John brings out another. Tag steps forward and gives him directions, as he has made the trip by stage.

"Will pay back," Mumu says, and he and Malani, her limping, head off to be first in line at the Hall and Crandall office at Mansion House at the corner of Clay and Kearney.

The others head out toward the Presidio, and I head the other direction, toward the Niantic Hotel. God willing, the Lord and Lady will have returned.

I've only met Lady Stanley-Smyth once, and barely had a conversation with her, but her reputation proceeds her as a philanthropist who's working to bring both an opera house and a city park to San Francisco. Let's hope her sympathies run to young women of Chinese extraction.

It takes me over twenty minutes to make the walk to the Niantic, but luckily the supper is over although the string quartet is still performing. The night maid fetches me a welcome cup of coffee as I await the Lord and Lady.

Appealing to him, he seems little interested, only concerned with my potential run-in with the law but calls Mrs. Stanley-Smyth over away from the group of friends. She's surprised to hear of the barracoon and immediately interested. After I spin the tale, she turns to her husband.

"Willard, this is an outrage and this young man and his friends are heroes. Please intercede immediately on his behalf. In fact, let's get Ogden in this conversation."

Without waiting she steps away and soon returns with a gentleman in tow with porkchop sideburns and a pearl stickpin in his four-in-hand tie.

She introduces me to Admiralty Judge Ogden Hoffman, then commands, "Jake, please tell your tale to Judge Hoffman."

When finished he says he'll take the matter up with Marshal Crozier in the morning and I soon find myself spinning the same tale to a Mr. Leland, who is the publisher of the *Weekly Pacific News*. He asks me if I can make some of the girls available for interview the next day, but before I can answer Mrs. Stanley-Smyth intervenes.

"Those young ladies will be under my care here at the hotel, then off to Sacramento to my newly established English Standard School for Young Ladies."

The Lord pulls me aside. "What's this matter about some gang posting flyers all over town?"

"I defended myself against three of them. Seems they took umbrage at my watching out for your shipment and causing the lot of those thieves to be fitted for shrouds."

"Then it's even more important you spend some time away from the city. The *Orient* is sailing with the tide at four fifteen this morning. You'll be on her."

"Gone for how long?" I ask.

"It's normally twenty to twenty-five days at sea, each way. Two months at least. That'll give this Wallaby thing time to cool down."

"Or I could have the *Windsong* drop me off at her most northerly point on this trip?"

"Jake, you signed on for five and a half trips. You're a pariah in San Francisco and this will keep you alive and out of reach of this rabble who call themselves Wallabys.

This will do for the last three and a half trips owed on the *Windsong*. Are you a man of his word?"

I sigh deeply but reply. "You know I am, sir."

"Fetch your gear from the *Windsong*, report to the *Orient*. I'm having Sam Wittsworth, one of my personal bodyguards, accompany you. There are two San Francisco policemen in the stable across the street, standing by because of this affair." He walks to the hotel desk and takes up quill, paper, and ink and writes a missive, calls the judge over, who signs it then returns and hands it to me. "This will protect you from the police. Take the two policemen stationed at the stable with you to find the girls from the barracoon and have the coppers bring them here to the hotel. Do the girls speak English?"

"One does, her name is Jaio."

"Fine, then you send them here with the two police escorts and you go straight to the ships. I'll look forward to seeing you upon your return."

"As you wish, sir."

Then a thought comes to me. "My friend, Mumu, is a Sandwich Islander. I wish he could sail with me."

"How do we find him?"

"He's at the express company Hall and Crandall, awaiting the morning stage to escort his sister, the reason we were at the barracoon in the first instance...to escort her safely to their family in Monterey."

"I'll send another man to escort her. He's a seaman?"

"He is. And a very good one. Not much on the booms but he's a bull on deck. As strong as one."

"Then he, too, will have a berth on the *Orient*, should he agree to accompany you."

It seems I'm off to enjoy the longest single ocean trip on earth without any possible landfall, across nearly half the wide Pacific to the lonely Sandwich Islands.

## 17

I WANTED TO GO FETCH MUMU MYSELF, BUT THE LORD insisted I head straight for the *Orient* with a quickly penned letter in hand. I'm accompanied by a fella called Digger, who is armed even better than myself, twice my size, and anything but loquacious, as all he's done is grunt since he was given instructions by the Lord to see me safely to the ship.

But first I must pick up my belongings and say fare-thee-well to those aboard the *Windsong*, and I'm a bit surprised it almost brings me to tears to do so. It's amazing how close one becomes to a crew you have grown to depend upon, particularly on one of these fairly small villages of wood afloat with no other humans in sight. I'm pleased that Captain Polkinghorn says I'm welcome back, maybe not as a second mate, but surely as a common seaman, and that he'll be pleased to continue my education. Even First Mate McGillicutty seems sorry to see me go.

I'm surprised and hopefully honored that Polkinghorn insists on writing what he said is a letter of introduction to the *Orient* captain. He seals it, so I know not if it's a scathing rebuke or complimentary. I do return the books he's loaned me, with the regret that I've only read them twice and was hoping for a third so the information would soak into my thick skull.

And what a ship the *Orient* is, over two hundred feet in length, over thirty wide, full three masts with her mainmast jointed three times, three sections of Sitka spruce reaching a height, if I'm any judge, of nearly one hundred feet. Unlike the *Windsong* she has a three-foot raised quarterdeck aft, and deckhouse surrounding the mainmast, reminding me of a 44-gun frigate we passed at sea. And although the *Orient* is not so nearly as well armed, she does carry a six-pounder starboard and port, and a pair of three-pounder swivel guns, four total, both forward and aft, which are shown to me on a quick deck tour by First Mate Fredrick Lattrell accompanied by Bosun and Master Ernest Owsley. I offer my letters of introduction to Lattrell but am instructed to save them for Captain Herschel Constantine.

I'm told the *Orient* crews thirty-five, including a ship's carpenter who doubles as ironsmith, a second cook who also doubles as baker, and to my great surprise we have two cabins of passengers.

I'm shown to the forecastle and for the time being, I hope just the time being, will bunk with the common sailors. It's not that I mind bunking with the common seamen, but I admit to being a bit spoiled having some officer's privileges. It seems the captain is ashore and not returning until we're ready to cast off, so until his orders I'm in a state of flux. I quickly stow my goods in a trunk at the foot of my narrow hammock, sandwiched between others with barely a foot between. My Sharps won't fit the trunk, so it finds itself wrapped in my clothes under my swinging sleeper. Almost as quickly as I can get my clothes changed and my canvas slippers donned, the call is for all hands. I've yet to say more than good morning to the other crew as we race for the deck.

Not knowing where I'll be assigned by the captain, Lattrell puts me with the starboard watch, then assigns me as coxswain on a jolly boat. My first command, I laugh to myself, and soon find that command is not all it's put up to be as I'm expected to man an oar and help hoist a heavy anchor overboard and retrieve it shortly thereafter.

Unlike the smaller *Windsong* we are put to work carrying a kedge anchor out a hundred yards, dropping it to the bottom, while those aboard winch the ship away from the dock. We retrieve the anchor and are given line to take it another hundred yards. After five of these fairly rigorous trips, we're clear of the many anchored and abandoned craft, return to the ship, and four of us and our jolly boat are hoisted aboard.

I did not see him come aboard but am happy to run into Mumu who's accepted his assignment aboard the *Orient* as a common seaman. And I'm pleased to hear he saw Malani off to Monterey with the escort of an assigned bodyguard, thanks to Lord and Lady Stanley-Smyth. He's also able to report that our four shipmates made it back to the *Windsong*. I spent a careful time explaining to the Lord what transpired in the barracoon and that one of our men—I didn't name him—was forced to fire his scattergun into a barracoon guard and the act was purely self-defense. Lord Stanley-Smyth and his missus declared us heroes and swore he'd take the matter up with the police and assured me there'd be no repercussions. I'd hate to return from the Sandwich Islands to find Tag swinging from a gallows.

Still, I breathe a sigh of relief as we pass through the narrows and leave San Francisco, disappearing in the mist, off our larboard stern.

---

I DON'T KNOW if Captain Constantine is trying to make some kind of point or if he's merely busy but, even though he's seen me working the deck, he does not ask for a face-to-face or to receive my letters of recommendation from the ship's owner, Lord Stanley-Smyth, or from my former captain, Luther Polkinghorn. I'm sure he thinks me a privileged interloper, and I guess in many ways that's true.

Finally, the third day at sea, I'm beckoned to the captain's quarters. I rap soundly three times on his closed door and receive the command through it. "Stand fast. I'll bade you enter soon enough."

So, I wait. Again, I think he's merely making a point. It seems coming aboard any ship with the favor of the owner, or command, is starting with a black mark. I'm a little surprised you don't immediately receive ten lashes. I'm parked there in the passageway for twenty minutes, the time accurately counted on the gold watch I received from Lord Stanley-Smyth. Then I get a single, "Enter." And do.

I stand with knit hat in hand while he peruses some charts on his desk, until he finally looks up. "Jake Zane. I understand you have some communication for me from your former captain and Stanley-Smyth."

"Sir," I respond and step forward and hand them, but he doesn't take them.

"On the desk. I'll review them later. Are you comfortable bunking with the crew?"

"I'm comfortable wherever you command me to bunk, sir."

With that he gives me a rather curious look. I expect he was expecting me to complain. I once complained to my father about a request and got my answer, a swift kick in the behind that almost lifted me off the ground and sent me on the way to accomplish my assigned chore. I don't complain to my superiors unless I'm ready to take my leave, and taking one's leave while far at sea would be a wet and risky business.

He clears his throat before continuing. "As I'm sure you've discovered, we have a first and second mate and a bosun who also serves as master. Bosun Ernest Owsley has a vacant bunk in his cabin. You'll serve as bosun mate second class and work stores under Owsley. He's a handy and sound sailor and has plenty to teach, and I'm sure with your short time aboard you have plenty to learn?"

"Yes, sir. Thank you, sir."

"Don't thank me. You'll earn it. You'll still report deck side when all hands are called. In that case you'll work under Lattrell on the starboard watch. Clear?"

"Yes, sir."

"You'll dine with the crew, but with Owsley, the carpenter, and sailmaker and their small table…except on the Sabbath. On that one day you'll dine with me, Owsley, the officers…and our passengers, the Tannenbaum family."

"My pleasure, sir."

"You're excused."

"Yes, sir," and I give him a perfunctory salute and spin on my heel. He stops me at the door.

"Zane, do you have any medical skills?"

"No, sir, other than what my ma taught me on the

plains with herbs and such. I've helped treat some arrow wounds and set a broke bone more'n once."

"Well, we have no plains' herbs aboard and it's damn unlikely we'll have any arrow wounds, but Owsley also serves as ship's medical officer as he was a medical student in the east. Between you and I he shot another student over some woman, an honest duel I understand, but was thrown out of school. Still, he has lots to teach so you might pay close attention to what he has to say on doctoring."

"Yes, sir."

"Go."

"Yes, sir."

And I'm off to find my new boss, roommate, tablemate, and teacher of all things stores and medical.

It should be an interesting voyage.

## 18

To say we have a cabin is a bit of an exaggeration. Our bunks measure five and a half feet long and two feet wide, meaning I'll sleep with legs folded, and the upper and lower each have only two feet of headroom. The space under the lower is divided so each man has space for his trunk. Then another two feet of open space between bunks and bulwark. The bulwark has six pegs upper and lower, but if one hangs his slicker it's covering the lower peg. A small shelf lines the open space at the end opposite our thin door, and the door boasts two hooks as well. The shelf has a rim so shaving mugs, brushes, straight razors, soap, or whatever won't go to the floor unless the captain has the ship heeled to the scuppers on the larboard side—not that many men shave.

The top bunk goes to me as Bosun Owsley has the preference, and the fact is I care little. My Sharps fits nicely between my thin mattress and the bulwark on the bunk side. As my scattergun breaks in half it fits in the trunk. I am nearing six feet tall, three or four inches taller than most the crew, so sleeping is constant turning and tossing. I feel privileged to have what little privacy the cabin allows, even though Owsley and I are normally on the same shift so "home" at the same time.

I immediately determine that Owsley is a strange sort. He answers most questions with a grunt and seldom talks unless instructing me of something, which is near constant. My hoped-for medical lessons are yet to surface.

The *Orient* boasts three decks. The upper, which is the floor of the quarterdeck and only the aft third of the ship, the main deck, and the lower which runs the length of the ship and separates the primary cargo area from the bilge. The bilge, in fact, is also a cargo area as it carries all the iron goods the ship hauls for trade with the Sandwich Islanders. Plow shears, spikes, nails, rails, kettles, and pots and pans. This is the ballast, weight necessary for keeping the ship upright and from being blown down by a gale. Should the return goods not be adequately heavy, we'll load the bilge with tons of beach rock. It's said that half the cobblestone streets of Boston, New York, and other eastern port cities are cobbled with rock ejected from returning vessels.

Before we are a week at sea, I am sick of my job below decks, tending stores, cargo, constantly making sure the ricking—wooden bracing—is tight and keeping cargo from shifting. Had I not developed my sea legs, I'd be seasick from never seeing the horizon, which orients a fellow. In the dark, it's the life of a bat. I long to be topside where I can enjoy the weather and open sea, even the hot sun, wind, and rain. And a horizon to make things right with the world.

I also find myself in the role of policeman, as the crew

is not above trying to slip below and help themselves to an extra mug of grog or even a biscuit or chunk of salt pork or fish. I am instructed to take a marlinspike to their noggin should I catch them thieving. Then report them so they'll receive a dozen lashes from Lattrell's cat-o'-nine-tails. The captain has a half-dozen cases of special French brandy and Irish whiskey which he keeps for his own table, but even more so for entertaining or gifts for those ashore, or even for trade goods. I am warned he keeps careful count on those bottles, noting it in his journal, and it will be my hide should any go missing. He also has a padlocked trunk loaded with cheeses, dried meats, salamis, headcheese, and dried fruit. Each time I report below I make a count so as to know if one or more cases have gone missing in my absence.

We're at sea well over a week before I have the pleasure of meeting our passengers, who are being given a tour of the ship by the captain.

The Right Reverend Orville Tannenbaum is a man of my height with a shock of gray hair sweeping back to nearly shoulder length. His wife, Margaret Ann, is a pretty woman with a ready smile—I wonder how sincere—who I'm told is a teacher. But it's the daughter who catches my eye, with sparkling blue eyes and wavy blonde hair to mid-back, rosy cheeks, and a flashing smile that would melt the heart of a weaker man. I'd guess Nancy Ann's age at a year younger than my now eighteen. It's hard to turn my attention to her younger brother, Toby, but his actions draw my attention particularly when Captain Constantine directs me to accompany him fore and aft. Unfortunately, when his sister asks to go along, she's snapped at by the reverend and instructed to remain beside her mother. I'm pleased to note she seems disappointed not to go on my conducted tour.

It's a good thing young Toby is talkative as I lathe the questions on as we go from lumber lift to crate to pile of trade goods and I explain.

"These are kegs of nails," I say, then add, "where are you folks from?"

"Boston. We tried to get a ship direct to the islands, but it was quite a wait and the reverend was worried about the yellow fever so we went on to San Francisco."

I had a smile to myself with the son calling his father "the reverend" and not "Pa" or "Father." But I ignore it and continue. "So, your ma is a teacher?"

"Yes, Mother will teach in Lahaina or wherever the reverend is assigned."

"And what will you do on the islands?" I ask.

"I will be my mother's best student, teach the savages about Jesus, and study the bird life. I plan to be an ornithologist and study all over the world."

He picks up a pry bar and starts to open a crate, and I snatch it out of his hand.

"Owwwww!" he yells, and his mother and sister come running. "This lout hurt me!" he says with a whine.

"I'm sorry, but he was—" I try to explain.

His mother snatches the bar out of my hand. "And what did you plan to do with that?"

"Stow it," I say.

She turns to her husband and Captain Constantine, with accusation in her tone, "This impudent whelp told me to 'stow it.'"

"That's not—" the daughter tries to explain. I see the amused smile on her face.

"Apologize!" the captain snaps at me.

So, I do. "I'm sorry, ma'am, but you misunderstood."

She's red in the face. "I understand perfectly. Were you my student you'd have a mouth full of lye soap for your impudence."

"Yes, ma'am."

"Return to your duty," the captain snaps.

Happy to escape, I walk to the other end of the hold and check ricking I've already checked.

They near me as they escape the hold and as the girl, Nancy Ann, ascends the ladder she turns, blinks beautiful blue eyes, and flashes a smile at me. I give her a salute and am impudent as I also wink. I think she blushes as she quickly moves on up the ladder. I catch a glance of a pretty ankle under her long skirt.

Her father, last on the ladder, gives me a look down his long nose that would melt candle wax, and he, too, gets a perfunctory salute.

Seems I've both made a friend and three potential adversaries. I have to wonder for a moment how wise it is to gain the dislike, or even the disdain, of a man of God. But then I remember my father telling me that we all have God's ear, equally, and He sees all. So, if true, He saw exactly what the arrogant Toby attempted without permission, and heard me say I was only going to stow the bar, not use it on Toby's nosy nose.

So, I'd prefer to be right with the Lord than right with his second fiddle.

And I'd much prefer to be right with one of his more nicely crafted creations, Miss Nancy Ann.

# 19

It's Sunday, the Sabbath, a day I'm scheduled to dine with the captain, officers, and passengers. I expect to be called before the captain to be instructed that I'm not welcome at the table and to dine with the crew.

So, I'm not surprised when Owsley appears at the head of the ladder and yells to me, "You're summoned to the captain's quarters."

I am surprised when he personally answers my knock and bides me sit across the desk. And with his sly smile.

"Seems you've settled in nicely, Mr. Zane."

"I hope my work satisfies, sir."

"Your work is more than adequate. Are you tiring of being below deck?"

"Truthfully, sir?"

"I wouldn't ask if I didn't want a sincere answer."

"It's a bit like being in a bat cave. The sun, or even the night stars would be a welcome change. You've only called all hands twice and given me a chance to breathe fresh air."

He laughs. "I once spent three months as stores mate. Some crave it, seems not you nor I."

"No, sir. But I do as ordered."

He gives me a satisfied nod, then a smile, then, "I had a good laugh with that stuffy minister's wife taking umbrage at your 'stow it.' That was almost good enough to put in my journal."

I take the liberty of a small smile. "You know it was one of your personal crates he took the liberty of trying to pry open."

"I do, and you did exactly the right thing. Were he my whelp I'd blister his backside but he's a passenger and they get a great deal of slack." He chuckles, then continues, "At the turn of the watch on the morrow you report to Lattrell. You're relieved of stores."

"Thank you, sir. Should I avoid the officers' table this evening?"

He laughs. "Hell no, just mind your manners as I know you will. I enjoy seeing the steam roil out of that stuffy woman's ears. In fact, I've asked the steward to sit you next to the daughter. Seems she took to you, to her ma's great dismay." And he laughs again.

"Then, sir, may I have time to go to my cabin. I'm due a shave and a bit of a scrub."

"Permission granted."

I rise and salute, and salute again before I exit his quarters. And hurry to mine, swinging by the deckhouse and kitchen as I do and talk the cook, McCallager, out of a half bucket of hot water.

I'm spit and polish at 17:30, and am ten minutes early at four bells, or six o'clock on the gold pocket watch Lord Stanley-Smyth gave me.

The captain, of course, is at the head of the table, which seats ten. First Mate Fredrick Lattrell is to his right, Second Mate Silas St. Keyne to his left. Silas is a solid sort, shorter by a half a head than myself, but thick and muscular. Next to him is shipmaster and Bosun Mate Ernest Owsley. I'm seated next to Lattrell. There are place cards at the passenger's seats. Miss Nancy Ann is next to me. Her younger brother Toby across and next to Owsley. Mother Margaret is next to Nancy Ann and the foot of the table hosts the Right Reverend Orville Tannenbaum.

Captain Constantine, St. Keyne, Lattrell, and I are seated as the passengers arrive. I'm first on my feet and snatch off my new straw.

"Welcome," the captain greets them, and he and the other shipmates stand. "While we're up, Reverend, would you honor us with grace."

As he, seeming automatic and rote rather than sincere, blathers on and on and our supper likely loses its heat, I can't help but quote my father who quoted Shakespeare, "Words without thoughts never to heaven go," but I wisely keep the quote to myself.

Captain Constantine, I think purposefully, yawns rather loudly, and the reverend takes the hint and we all follow him with an "Amen." And take our seats. The captain introduces me alone as it seems the others have been dining together every evening.

I mumble, "Nice to meet you," and catch the eye of each of the guests, and the scowl of all but Nancy Ann. I have to catch my breath as her knee presses to mine and she gives me a mischievous smile and nod.

I carefully watch them all and take my cues from them, maintaining my silence as they chat, until Nancy Ann turns to me. "And where do you hail from, Mr. Zane?"

Clearing my throat, I answer, "Near St. Joe, Missouri,

then the Oregon Trail to a rough plot of land we turned into a farm near the Snake River in Oregon, then on back trails to San Francisco where I was blessed to be hired onto the *Orient*."

Mrs. Tannenbaum speaks before Nancy Ann can reply. "You actually think service aboard a rat-infested vessel a blessing. Seems, young man, your judgment of blessings is as poor as your choice of words."

Captain Constantine comes to my rescue before I can reply. It's a good thing as I am considering my words carefully before I speak. And none of them are complimentary.

"Madam," the captain says, his mouth in a slight smile but his eyes flashing fire. "We take great pride in the condition of our ship and value our cats greatly as they keep the rats at bay."

It's all I can do not to add, "But not the very large ones," but don't.

The reverend speaks before she can reply. "Now, Margaret, we've not seen a rat in our quarters, and you must value the *Orient* for providing our, so far, uneventful trip to the islands." Then he turns his attention to the captain. "You'll pardon the missus and her sharp tongue. She's been off her appetite with the rolling of the ship and all."

Constantine chuckles. "Well, sir, you might ask the Almighty to take pity on your missus, as I fear the rolling of the ship has just been a slight prelude to the next few days. Our barometer has fallen several points in the last few hours. I suspect before morning we'll be reefing sail."

Then the cook and his mate arrive with a platter of fried fish; seems one of the hands has been trailing lines and hooked more than one dolphin, called dorado in California, mahi-mahi in other places. Next to it the mate places a platter of potatoes, carrots, and turnips. Bread, seemingly just out of the oven, arrives and a bowl of churned butter is placed next to it. They return to the kitchen and the cooks mate returns with a pitcher of wine and starts with the reverend, who seems grateful to receive a mug full. His missus refuses with a grimace and outstretched hand. Toby and Nancy Ann are passed by. I receive a special furrowed brow from the missus when I accept a mug full.

I wait for her dressing down, and again feel Nancy Ann's knee against my outer thigh. Missus Tannenbaum couldn't harangue me enough to make me unhappy at the moment.

## 20

BUT ALL I GET FROM THE REVEREND'S WIFE IS A SOUR glare.

A knee against my thigh, a fetching glance, a meal that makes me want to dance and sing...a sour look could hardly sadden me.

I've been living on hardtack, lobscouse, and duff—a pudding of salt meat, dried fruit, and molasses—beans, mush, rice, salted fish and salt pork since leaving port, so I have no trouble staying quiet as I shovel it in as fast as maintaining a polite demeanor will allow. The meal is followed by a pudding, the fruit of which I can't identify, but it's sweet and delicious and sweetened with real sugar rather than blackstrap molasses which is bitter and sweet at the same time.

The fact that Toby remains silent is a surprise to me, I get a glare or two from the young man, but wonder if his sister might have dressed him down for his causing me to have to apologize for something I didn't do? Then he pushes the pudding away half eaten. And complains, "Too gooey."

When all are sated and the table cleared, the cook's mate again arrives, this time with several stem glasses and a decanter, and all but the ladies and Toby are poured three fingers of brandy. He's followed in by one of the crew, Charley O'Donnell, carrying a fiddle, and soon we enjoy a rousing rendition of "Consider the Lilies" then "Molly Bawn."

Missus Tannenbaum does not applaud but does make a request. "Young man, I don't suppose you have any hymns in your songbook?"

"Ma'am, how about 'Be Kind to Your Loved Ones at Home'?"

"That's hardly a hymn, young man."

I can't help but speak up as I know the song. "It's not exactly a hymn, but appropriate while here at sea." I look at each of them in turn, and linger on Nancy Ann, as I recite the last verse:

> "Be kind to thy sister not many may know
> The depth of true sisterly love;
> The wealth of the ocean lies fathoms below
> The surface that sparkles above.
> Be kind to thy father, once fearless and bold,
> Be kind to thy mother so near;
> Be kind to thy brother, nor show thy heart cold,
> Be kind to thy sister so dear."

I'm pleased with another beautiful smile and nudge of a knee from Nancy Ann who almost whispers, "That was lovely, Jake. Thank you."

I get an envious glare from O'Donnell, I guess angry I've stolen some attention from his entertaining.

"A hymn, please," the missus asks, but it's more a snarled demand than request.

The captain makes a request. "How about 'Abide with Me,' Charley. I know you know that one."

"I'm sorry, Capt'n," Charley replies. "You said happy or I'd have played it."

"Go ahead, with a storm 'bout to lay us down, it's appropriate."

Charley is not only a fiddler, but a singer of some repute. I've heard him on deck leading more than one chantey. He begins, his voice rather haunting:

> *Abide with me; fast falls the eventide;*
> *The darkness deepens; Lord with me abide.*
> *When other helpers fail and comforts flee,*
> *Help of the helpless, O abide with me.*
>
> *Swift to its close ebbs out life's little day;*
> *Earth's joys grow dim; its glories pass away;*
> *Change and decay in all around I see;*
> *O Thou who changest not, abide with me.*
>
> *Not a brief glance I beg, a passing word,*
> *But as Thou dwell'st with Thy disciples, Lord,*
> *Familiar, condescending, patient, free.*
> *Come not to sojourn, but abide with me.*
>
> *Come not in terror, as the King of kings,*
> *But kind and good, with healing in Thy wings;*
> *Tears for all woes, a heart for every plea.*
> *Come, Friend of sinners, thus abide with me.*

Charley plays another couple of bars without singing, then stops and begs off. "Sorry, folks, that's all the verses I know."

"A cheerful little tune," Lattrell says with a chuckle.

The he adds, "I hope this storm comes not in terror, and that the abide with me doesn't mean at His side before our time."

"How about a game of whist?" the captain asks.

"We are to bed," Missus Tannenbaum announces.

And Nancy Ann adds, "Thank you, Captain, for a fine meal. It was delicious."

"It was adequate," her mother adds, as they stand.

After the passengers excuse themselves, I figure it's my cue to leave. "May I be excused, sir. New duty in the morning will likely take all my well-rested attention."

"And sure footedness," Lattrell adds, and I take it as a warning I'll be high off the deck, and that with a storm trying to put me in the cold briny.

"We have enough for a game," the captain says, "cook will join us," and waves me away.

I only have three hours before Owsley will yell me awake, and when he does it seems as if I'd just closed my eyes. I'm wondering if I should have sipped that three fingers of brandy to the bottom as I pull on the canvas slippers Mumu made for me, then think it again as Owsley advises, "Take your slicker. She's blowing and cold as a banker's heart. Damn if it ain't supposed to be summer."

It's as dark as a foot up a bull's butt when I top the deck, salt spray slaps me in the face as its blowing horizontal, and I see First Mate Luttrell standing, leaning into the wind, eyes upward, hands on his hips. He turns and shouts an order, but the wind's howling and I don't hear. I take five strides to his side and cup an ear and he repeats, "Take a coil of repair line and join Peterson on the mizzenmast top rail. The topgallant halyard has parted and needs mending. She's full reefed and slack so now's the time."

"Yes, sir," I yell and head aft to the smallest of the masts, I'm happy to say as it likely means working, at most, sixty feet off the deck rather than one hundred. Not that sixty feet won't kill you dead as a fileted mackerel. I need to get my sea legs under me again, as you lose the feel of ropes under your feet when working stores below for over a week. As instructed, I grab a coil of one-inch hemp from a deck box and loop it over my shoulder. It's on the heavy side so inhibits my climb somewhat.

I'm halfway up the mizzen shrouds, the ratlines, when, even over the roar of the wind, the creak of timbers, and the slapping of halyards against masts and yardarms, I hear the scream above me.

Peterson has slipped and is hanging; the halyard has, thank God, taken a half hitch around his ankle. He's swinging like a clock's pendulum, arms flailing, and screaming like a cat with his tail under Grandpa's rocker.

I take a deep breath, chuck the line off my shoulder, and let it fly to the deck, and climb like the devil was on my tail.

I'm all that stands between Peterson living or us having to holystone his blood and brains off the deck.

## 21

I'VE NEVER MOVED WITH AS MUCH CARELESS ABANDON ON the ratlines, but am sure-footed as a cat, surprising in the howling wind and splattering rain. Reaching a spot opposite him, I await his swing until I can reach out and get a handful of his slicker and pull him near. He's hanging upside down but I'm able to encircle a thigh and pull him close. He madly reaches for the ratlines and his eagerness is not well served as he knocks my right foot free and for a thrashing moment, I fear we're both taking our last dive to the deck.

    I recover my footing and he wraps me as tight as a spider's web binding a fly, and when he does it takes the weight off the leg about which the halyard has taken the half hitch. It loosens and swings free, and suddenly all his weight is on my right arm and we both slip two spaces on the ratlines. Fortune smiles on me as my feet land firmly on the third ratline. He gathers the lines in a tight grip below my footing, and before we both go, I yell, "You got hold, I'm turning your leg loose."

It's a moment before he calms enough to reply, "I got a good hold, lemme go."

I do, and his legs swing out and down but now one arm is entangled in a ratline, as he fell and spun it took a turn on his wrist.

"Owww," he cries out. "My wrist, my wrist!"

"Get your footing. I'm cutting you free." I pull my folding knife from my pocket, assure myself he's got good footing and not hanging only by the well-secured wrist, and confirm so. "Are you square?"

"Hurry, it's cutting the blood off."

So, I saw away and now we have a ratline to repair as well as a halyard.

As I watch him wrap both arms around the lines and he's madly rubbing the wrist, I notice that two other sailors from the larboard watch have started up to join us. I don't remember a time when help was more welcome.

The two rescuers adeptly swing to the underside of the ratlines and pass us like monkeys. One has the coil of line I'd let fly over his shoulder. The fellow trailing yells back at me. "Mate wants you deck side. Lead so's you can help Pete."

To lead I have to pass Peterson to get below him. I presume so if he falls again, he'll have me as a backstop. I carefully pick my way down, his heels in my face, making sure each of his footfalls are solid.

Luttrell meets us at the deck and waves to the deck-house and we follow him inside. He yells to the cook. "Hot tea, or soup if you got it, Cookie."

And I say a silent prayer that he's not McGillicutty from the *Windsong*, who I'm sure would be ripping us up one side and down the other. First Mate Luttrell actually pulls out a stool for Peterson. "What happened?" he asks as Peterson flops down, still rubbing his wrist.

"Don' know, sir. Wind gust and suddenly I was downside up. Thank the good Lord that halyard grabbed holt of me."

He turns to me. "Good job, Zane. For a minute there I thought we'd be sewing you two in sailcloth."

"As did I," I say, glancing upward at the heavens.

"I've got to get back on watch." Luttrell turns to the cook, who I'd learned was called Pickles by some, Cookie by most.

"Pickles, a half measure of grog each for these two, then send them off." Then to me. "You report back deck side when your cup is drained, and I'll put you to eyeing the shrouds for damage for the rest of your watch."

"Yes, sir."

"Peterson, make sure Owsley looks you over so I don't have to run a needle through your nose to make sure you're dead, then feed you to the fishes."

"Yes, sir, Mr. Lattrell. Thank you, sir."

The grog, rum cut with water, is not normally to my liking but this cup was manna from heaven, warming me from tonsils to toenails.

I return to watch, happy not to be one of those aloft. As I walk the taffrail, careful not to have a gust take me to visit the whales, I eye a strange lump near the ladderway to below the quarterdeck, and approach to see what has been placed there. I am more than a little surprised when it moves and a flap near the top is flipped aside by a hand that suddenly appears. Blue eyes and soggy blond bangs eye me.

"Mr. Zane," I think she says, and I kneel beside her, my mouth close to her ear so she can hear.

"Miss Nancy Ann, are you applying for a common sailor's position?" And I laugh.

She brings those red lips nearer my ear. "No, smarty, I'm escaping my horrible brother." She pauses a moment, then adds, "Do you think it a terrible sin to hate your brother?"

"Maybe as much as Cain hated Able, but with two sisters myself I can tell you they often wanted to hold my head deep in the cow trough."

"I hate him," she states flatly.

"My ma often told me, when I was distressed, 'This too will pass.' And by the gods it always seemed to. She's a very smart lady."

She is silent for a moment, then gives me a coy smile and brings her mouth even closer to my eager ears. So close I can feel her warm breath in the cold. "Did anyone ever tell you, you're a very sweet boy?"

I have to laugh a little at that. "Not since I gained my majority. It would now be a very sweet man, not that I wouldn't prefer called something more manly."

Now she laughs. "So, you prefer sour to sweet?"

"No, ma'am, sweet will suit me, coming from you."

"Already you value my opinion?"

"I don't take long to judge folks. Sometimes it's merely a smile at the right time gains my favor, and at the wrong time my dislike. Your ever-so-slight smile when your ma was trying to get me run up a yardarm was nicely timed and appreciated."

"I better return before my brother runs to Mama with tales of my absence."

"Let me go ahead, hands on my shoulders, please."

And I lead her to her and her brother's door.

She says, "Thank you, sweet Jake," very quietly as she closes the door.

With the door closed, I can hear her brother Toby, "Jake? Pa is going to skin your hide."

Even if we're both under the lash, I must keep her thinking what a sweet soul I am, if I am. Again, Master Shakespeare comes to mind. "A woman would run through fire and water for such a kind heart." I remember something my mother told me when she saw me eyeing a neighbor girl. It was: "Remember always, 'A woman eyes a man with marriage in mind, a man eyes a woman with a mind easily read... Even if you find it difficult, keep your thoughts difficult to read.'"

Her father wouldn't think my thoughts so kind, so I must heed my mother's advice.

The storm doesn't let up and even with my experience on the ratline I am kept topside as all hands are called. I've been topside ten hours when finally told I can take a dogwatch, six hours, I hope of uninterrupted sleep.

It is not to be. Owsley awakens me with a punch to the shoulder. "You're summoned to the captain's quarters. Now!"

## 22

Surprised, I have to cover my eyes with a hand to stave off the bright sun. And it's a sailor's fair wind, not a gale.

I am only slightly less surprised to find both Reverend and Missus Tannenbaum in attendance when I enter.

"Sir," I address the captain.

"Stand at attention, Zane."

"Aye, sir."

"Young Toby says you laid hands on Miss Nancy Ann."

I can't help myself. "Storms often cause one to have nightmares, sir."

"Don't be flippant, young man," the missus snaps. She is only slightly less red in the face than the reverend.

"I'm not, ma'am. If I'm being accused of something, shouldn't my accuser and the alleged victim be in attendance?"

Of course, the reverend had to add his two bits. "I

think you an evil young man, and for that you should be punished."

I feel my face heating and my hackles rising. I hadn't liked this man from my first sighting. I try to keep my voice level. "I presume you know your Bible, sir?"

"That's an impudent question," Missus snaps and the reverend clamps his jaw. It seems she does know her Bible, and says, "Flee the evil desires of youth and pursue righteousness, faith, love and peace, along with those who call on the Lord out of a pure heart."

I clear my throat and search my memory for the quote I want. "Perhaps this is more for your son than yourselves, however, thou shalt not raise a false report, put not thine hand with the wicked to be an unrighteous witness."

That gets the dogs out from under the porch, and the reverend jumps to his feet and his voice is quaking. "Damn you, you arrogant nit, quoting the Bible to a Right Reverend." He takes a step forward as if he's going to try and punch me.

Captain Constantine's sharp rebuke stops him short. "Tannenbaum, take a seat."

The reverend is so angry he's quaking like an aspen, and I wonder if the missus is going to have apoplexy and pass out.

Then the captain turns to me. "Zane, your words, not the Bible. What happened last night."

"I discovered Miss Nancy Ann on deck, wrapped in a man's oilskin, hunkered down as if she had no place to go. We had a short conversation and I accompanied her to her cabin door and stood by to make sure she safely entered."

"That's it?" the captain asks.

"That's not—" the missus begins but the captain stops her short.

"Please have your son and daughter report to my quarters. I'll talk with them."

The Tannenbaums stand, and the reverend glowers down at the seated captain. "I will bring them—"

But he doesn't get it out. "You may bring them, but you'll stay outside while I have a conversation with them," and he turns to me, "You're excused, Zane."

"Yes, sir. Thank you, sir."

As I'm closing the captain's door, I hear both the Tannenbaums argue, "That's not proper. She's a young—"

And closing the door, I can hear no more. As I exit the ladder onto the main deck, Nancy Ann and Toby are standing near the scuttlebutt; she's sipping a ladle of water. As I pass, I smile at Toby. "Shoat, if you were my size both your eyes would be black as ebony and likely closed to an eighth inch. I can't abide liars." I stomp on by.

As I move away, I hear Nancy Ann behind me. "And I'd bloody your nosy nose."

―――

I'M AGAIN RELEGATED to dining with the crew, but at a small separate table with Owsley, the ship's carpenter Alex Tobias, and sailmaker Thomas Hitchcock. As we finish our bowl of beans and molasses, the fiddle player from the night before—Charley, as I recall—wanders over with two other common sailors close behind and braces me without so much as a "good morning."

"You must be the captain's lackey, dining with him

and the hoity-toity passengers. You his sodomite, or what?"

That's said as he stands near behind me.

Laughter comes from the twelve-seat table behind him.

I dab my mouth with my kerchief, stand slowly, turn, and break his nose with a straight right hand with lots of anger behind it. He bounces off other seated sailors and crashes to the deck, flat on his back. Blood gushes out of his nose. The other two step in and we trade blows but with my anger feel nothing and give as good as I get until my three table mates step in, Owsley being the superior officer, and stop the brawl. The smaller table is turned over, wooden bowls and spoons and grub are scattered about. Cookie is standing with a meat cleaver in hand, shaking it at all of us as if he's about to go to lopping heads off.

All of the combatants are bleeding from nose or lips or cut eyebrows, and all panting like they've raced to the highest yardarm. One of my eyes is swelling shut and know will be dark as a ripe plum, but I'm happy to observe a split lip on one of the others and a bleeding nose on his partner.

Owsley, being the highest ranking, commands, "Damn you, insulting a man trying to peacefully fill his gullet before returning to work." As he talks, he kneels, tears a patch off of Charley O'Donnell's shirt, and on one knee before the dazed fiddler, stuffs his nose with wads of patch.

I'm happy he snaps at the others and not me, "You three will pass your grog for three days." Then he grabs O'Donnell by the jaw and shakes him. "You hear me?" And gets a small nod. "You'll meet Zane atop a box when your nose stops gushing for some entertainment for the crew."

"But...but...but my nose," he sputters.

"Blows to body only will be the rule."

"Atop a box?" I ask, not knowing the term.

"Aye, boxing, as it's known on a frigate. To settler grudges. Any man knocked off the box three times is the loser. And that's the end of it. Should he start another ruckus he'll get the lash. Understand?"

And I nod. It's nearly more words than I've heard from Owsley since I've been aboard. However, I think it hardly fair as O'Donnell won't be himself for a long time. Owsley moves his head back and forth, then reaches down with both hands, and with O'Donnell's nose between pressed palms, resets it with a crack.

"Owww, you son of a whore," O'Donnell screams, grabbing Owsley's wrists with both hands, but his nose is straight again. He's gushing blood as one of the wads has shot free, but straight.

"Be still!" Owsley commands and restuffs the wad. Then he turns to me. "Back to work. I have to clear the box with the cap'n."

One of the sailors, a burly fellow with a full head of curly black hair to match his beard mumbles, "Ain't over, sodomite. A fella could get bumped over the rail."

Owsley hears the man and snaps, "No grog for a week, Odergaard. And you better hope Zane doesn't go over the rail as I'll sink my marlinspike to your spine or you'll swing from a yardarm."

I knew this peaceful life aboard was too good to be true.

## 23

I'm not a bit surprised to be on deck, ready to mount the ratlines on the big mainmast when I'm beckoned to the captain's quarters.

I enter to find Owsley and O'Donnell already there standing before the captain's chart table. He looks up.

"Zane, we damn near made the Islands without some fuss. Should sight them on the morrow. I understand you and O'Donnell here had a misunderstanding?"

"I guess you could call it that, sir."

"And Owsley has suggested a deck box to settle the matter."

"Whatever the custom, sir."

He turns to O'Donnell. "Will that settle the matter, seaman?"

"Hardly fair, sir. My nose being broken and all."

"The bosun has suggested body blows only. Any man who hits above the shoulders will receive five lashes." And he turns back to me. "Understand, Zane?"

"Yes, sir."

"It's been my ardent hope we'll remain a friend ship, but it is as it is. So, get on with it."

We all reply at the same time, "Yes, sir."

The captain orders, "Tomorrow will be a busy day, so settle this now. Pipe all hands, bosun."

"Yes, sir," Owsley replies.

Owsley holds the door for all, and we salute and exit.

As we head for the deck, I question Owsley, "And the rules for this boxing thing?"

"No gouging the eyes. No biting. No fists or knees to the family sack. And that's it. You're knocked off the box three times you lose and it's all over. You don't start the battle until I yell 'Fight.' Understand?"

"Yes, sir."

My pa gave me plenty of lessons in fisticuffs, but that was on flat ground and no-holds-barred. This seems some different as the only two deck boxes on the main deck are four feet wide and six long, so not much room for a kick or back step.

We don't ascend the two-foot-high box until all hands are gathered. I can hear the men grumble that it's an unfair match as O'Donnell has one eye badly swollen and his nose is twice its width. The fact is my left eye is half closed, but I guess that's not worth a mention. I hear men, consequently, trying to bet on me but there are no takers. Seems they judge O'Connell's condition far worse. I, too, have decided the match anything but fair as I'm a half-head taller, at least as heavy, and maybe fifteen years younger than the fiddle player.

As we're led to the box, a man yells out, "Don't break his fingers, sogger. We need the music."

I give him a nod. As I mount the box I glance up to atop the quarterdeck and see the Tannenbaum family lined up. Nancy Ann's mother is saying something, trying to push her daughter away from the match, but she's adamant about staying.

We square away atop the box and I don't realize that I'm against the edge with my heels and O'Donnell is near the middle. A man in the crowd yells, "Sodomite," and I glance over just as Owsley yells, "Fight!"

Before I can raise my fists, O'Donnell has taken a step and his right glances off my chin and my backward reflex step sends me sprawling to the deck amid thirty or more laughing men. I know I redden, not from being struck as the blow did little, but from embarrassment.

This time Owsley makes sure both of us have our heels on the edge.

He yells "Fight!"

And we both step forward as O'Donnell swings a wild roundhouse punch which I easily duck and which throws him off balance, and rather than drive a hard punch to his belly I give him a push with both hands and he flies into the arms of his supporters, off the box.

I hear moans from the men, I guess not approving of my tactics, but breaking the ribs of a man already injured would give me no satisfaction.

At the next "Fight" he lowers his head and charges, I guess hoping to butt me off the box, but I drop even lower and his upper torso bends over my back, and I stand erect and hoist his legs and over he goes, hitting the deck hard as his boys don't bother to catch him.

The breath is knocked out of him, and he lays there a minute before others help him to his feet. I can see he's done in so turn to Owsley. "Is there any conceding?"

"No," he snaps, and they help O'Donnell up on his end of the box.

I think they think I meant will O'Donnell concede, but I don't, I mean I'd be happy to concede rather than see the poor man hit the deck again and possibly be hurt badly.

This time he charges and again I drop a shoulder and he goes over my back, but rather than throw him I jump off the box carrying him with me.

"Two for me, three for O'Donnell," I say, as I set him back on his feet.

The crowd yells its disapproval and O'Donnell tries another roundhouse punch to my chin. I merely step back and his punch swishes the air.

"Damn you, damn you," he mutters, but he's finished and knows it.

Owsley steps forward. "That's five lashes for you, O'Donnell," he says, and seems happy to do so.

"But he missed," I offer.

"Not for this try, he put one on your chin when he knocked you off."

I think a second, then say, "My fault, he swung for the chest and I blocked him up into my chin."

Owsley studies me a moment. Then offers, "I didn't see it that way." But O'Donnell's chums, overhearing, offer agreement.

"That's right. No lashes." But they now, seeing I'm trying to avoid O'Donnell the lash, seem sympathetic to my case and yell, "A fair fight, done and over." And begin to wander away.

I glance up at the quarterdeck taffrail but the Tannenbaums have left the sorry exhibition.

We've been twenty-three days at sea, and the Sandwich Islands are a spot of gray on the horizon. We've had a fairly uneventful trip. A two-hundred-plus-foot ship with thirty-five crew plus four passengers is a blessing to freight and those rigged for it, to passengers. It's also a curse ofttimes when a man is seriously injured or worse, lost at sea. Only one week of inclement weather, and it never exceeding a Force Five wind and waves no more than ten or twelve feet, is more than a mere blessing.

I've not been called to the captain's quarters for a dressing down or a pat on the noggin, which is how I'd like to keep it. I also have not had a chance to trade smiles with Miss Nancy Ann Tannenbaum, as yesterday, after my boxing expedition, I was informed it better if I dine with the crew rather than my Sunday invite to the officer's table.

Eager would be a great understatement in regard to my first view of somewhere other than the U.S. of A. or former Mexican territory along the Oregon Trail, now part of the U.S. but a territory rather than state. I've seen my share of natives, having been shot at by some and having shot at plenty. I lost a half-dozen trail friends and workmates on my last sojourn, hopefully these islanders are more friendly.

As the islands come nearer, and the sun nears the western horizon, the Tannenbaums come topside to view the approach of their new home. Luckily, I've been assigned cargo duty, assuring all's secure and ready to be off-loaded, and it's deck cargo I'm to attend. Not the bat cave. The passengers are lined up main deck forward and move off to look over the bow. Miss Nancy Ann, seeing me nearby, falls behind and lets them go ahead and unnoticed, then slips over beside me.

"That was kind of you to spare that man more embarrassment."

"Ma'am?"

"The man on the box. I was proud of you for doing all you could not to injure him more."

I laugh. "How do you know he just wasn't being kind to me."

"Don't be modest, Jake Zane. A kind heart, and I know you have one, accepts compliments."

"Yes, ma'am—"

"Yes, but not ma'am, Nancy Ann if you please."

"You'll be in trouble when the Right Reverend realizes you're not in tow."

She gets a bit wistful. "Will I ever see you again?" she asks, and I swear she's about to shed a tear.

Before I can answer she shoves me back so the mainmast is between us and the eyes of her family, nearly out of sight forward, and plants the sweetest of kisses on my surprised lips.

She backs away and challenges me. "We are to be stationed at Lahaina, the old whaling village which my father will use as a base for trips to the outer islands to continue to convert the savage. You're to come calling on me, no matter my parents' wishes."

I know I'm blushing with the kiss but am as forward with my reply. "And if they won't let you see me?"

"They can't watch my every moment. Papa plans to go immediately to outer islands to visit those already in his flock. If you have the slightest chance, before your return sail to San Francisco, come be by my side for a while. If not, come back. I will write you, general delivery, San Francisco."

It's a promise I don't feel I can make. "If it's in the stars."

She looks a bit disappointed, so I add, "Your suitors will be lined up for a mile, Nancy Ann. You'll soon forget me."

"No, Jake Zane, I will not. Back east one courts for a year or more. So, no matter who comes calling, I'll be without a ring on my hand for that much time or more.

I'll make no commitment until I'm sure you're not on the horizon."

"And I'll be, if it's in the stars. I understand hundreds of sailors, mostly whalers, visit Lahaina. And there are few ladies of quality. As I said, they'll be lined up all the way into the surf."

"A sailor is not my idea of a husband, and I'm sure you have much more in mind."

"You've read my mind," I reply, with a sincere smile.

With a shout from her father's gruff voice, she spins on a heel and heads forward. I feel a bit of a quandary. My first love, now in Oregon, has no idea I still have her in my heart. In fact, as it goes on the prairie, she may have wed the week she arrived on the Willamette River. Nancy Ann is now there as well, in my mind and heart. The Bard comes to mind, now that I mentioned if it resides in the stars, "Stars are fire, Doubt that the sun doth move his aides, Doubt truth to be a liar, but never doubt I love." Two beautiful, sweet, ladies have given me a flutter of beautiful long lashes, leaving me truly confused.

24

THESE ISLANDS ARE AS BEAUTIFUL AS REPUTED TO BE. As we sail near, some spots are so green they nearly hurt the eyes, and some barren with fresh lava flows. Pa often told me that things seem to even up, if a place seems beautiful look out for the snakes, if the weather perfect one day, a tornado is likely in the offing. So as beautiful as these islands seem to be, I notice a tendril of smoke from the high mountain, the largest mountain volcano I understand is called Mauna Kea and rises to nearly fourteen thousand feet elevation. And it's one of many on the islands.

The captain has given us a quick lesson on the Sandwich Island archipelago which consists of eight major islands, several atolls, and numerous smaller islets extending fifteen hundred miles from the Big Island of Hawaii northeast. We'll see only a small part of the island group.

We are to stop and trade at a port called Honolulu on a smaller island, Oahu—passing a planned stop at Lahaina on the island of Maui to do so. Honolulu is the capital of the kingdom led by King Kamehameha III. Then we're back to the island of Maui, the town of Lahaina—formerly a capital of the nation—to trade at the old whaling port and drop off our passengers. We plan to take on sugar, sandalwood, coconuts—both whole and dried—and dried salted fish. For those items we'll trade iron nails, plow shears, rails and spikes, and milled lumber.

I've barely seen Mumu on the crossing but meet up with him when called to the captain's quarters. Accustomed to standing in the captain's presence, I'm surprised when he asks both of us to take a seat.

The captain begins, "You are longtime friends, I understand?"

"Not so long, sir," I reply, "but very good friends I hope."

Mumu nods his big head. "Very good friends, very good mates. I owe much to Mr. Jake."

The captain turns to Mumu, "You were born on the islands?"

"Hana, sir."

"I need the absolute truth. You have no crimes or reason for the king or his cabinet to fear or dislike you."

Mumu merely stares for a moment, then stumbles a little as he answers. "Kamehameha my king. My mother's distant cousin…a distant cousin is Queen Kalama, his blessed wife. I would give life and all I possess to my king."

"You speak passable English and I understand the king is fluent?"

"It is so."

"So, please correct me if I'm wrong." And he turns to me. "I trust you, Zane, and am sending you on an important task."

"My pleasure, sir," I respond.

"Just in case you have language problems, I'm sending Akamu Ka Ana Ana with you to make sure there are no misunderstandings."

I'm slightly confused as I don't think I've ever heard Mumu's full name. Then, as he's nodded Mumu's way while speaking his name, I get it. And I nod.

"It is a simple task, but it's been my experience that simple tasks at times go awry." He pauses a moment and I'm on the edge of my chair, then only a little disappointed as he continues. "I have a case of fine French brandy you're to deliver to the palace, with my thanks for being welcomed to his kingdom."

"Sir, that seems simple enough."

"Please convey my sorrow that it's French. As you may know, a little over a year ago some frog of a French admiral, Tromelin, invaded Honolulu and sacked and looted the city, which served the U.S. well as soon after the king sought a treaty with us. Tell him, or his representative, whomever you're allowed to see, that I would have preferred bringing him some good American whiskey, but San Francisco was drank dry of a decent bottle when I went to procure his gift. You got all that, Zane?"

"Yes, sir. Perfectly."

"We'll tie up at Waikiki near zero nine hundred hours and you're to set out immediately. It's my hope he'll invite me to call on him, so assure him or his representative I'll be honored to do so."

"Yes, sir," I say, and Mumu nods.

"If you don't meet the king, you'll likely get an audience with an expatriate American, Gerrit Judd, who's a close adviser to the king."

I clear my throat. "Pardon me for asking, but why aren't you going yourself?"

"Politics, young man. Having an underling refused an audience with the king rather than an American ship captain saves face. Years ago, the Exploring Expedition, five ships mapping the Pacific, called on the king and caused America some embarrassment. We walk lightly since."

"I guess I understand," I reply.

"Fight shy of politics, young man. You'll be better off in the long run." He gives me a smile and nod. "Now, you're both free of duty until your task in the morning. Mr. Zane, take Mumu to your quarters and he'll teach you the customs and basic language of the islands, such as thank you, excuse me, hello, goodbye…like that. Learn well, I don't want to hear of a mistake or your part insulting the king or his cabinet…or any islander for that matter."

"Yes, sir," I say and we both give a salute and leave.

When we reach the main deck Second Mate Silas St. Keyne beckons us over and orders me up the mizzenmast.

"Sorry, sir, but the captain has ordered us both below where I'm to get a lesson in island customs."

He glares at me. "What the hell for? You a bloody diplomat or what?"

I try not to smile as that seems a fair question. "No, sir, on an errand for the captain the instant we tie up. I guess he doesn't want me to embarrass the ship or himself."

"Ridiculous," he stammers, then adds with resignation, "get your sogger ass below."

I salute, "Sir," and we head for the ladder.

Surprisingly, Mumu has a great depth of knowledge

about the islands of his birth. You'd expect him to know the flora, fauna, and geography, things any native would know of his land. But his knowledge of its history and government is amazing to me.

Brit James Cook is credited with the first European discovery of the islands in the late seventeen hundreds, about the same time as the American Revolution. That said, Spain claimed the discovery two centuries before. But it was Cook who brought great change as he introduced firearms which allowed the then King Kamehameha the First to conquer and unify the rest of the islands and, thus, unify the kingdom. Even more radical changes came with American Protestant missionaries and the new worldliness of native islanders who crewed on whaling vessels and were exposed to the rest of the world. Following closely behind the missionaries and conversion of islanders to Christianity were sugar farmers who introduced sugarcane. Now it was not only whalers and sandalwood traders calling on the island, but those seeking sugar, in great demand the world over and particularly in California and Oregon, so hard to reach by ships from the Caribbean islands where cane is also grown. Five of every six whaling ships that call on the islands are from New York or Boston, so the American influence is great.

Mumu seems almost embarrassed to inform me that the islanders and immigrants quickly learned how to separate the sailors from their own hard-earned, and plenty of saloons feature whiskey and whores, much to the chagrin of the missionaries. Mumu refers to other sailors, particularly whalers, as jackanapes and vulgar upstarts.

All this influence from the U.S. brought new government and American advisers…and it also brought a substantial reduction in population. European disease halved the population of the islands from over three hundred thousand prior to Captain Cook to just over eighty thousand now. The native population is being supplemented by the immigration of both Chinese and Japanese, who work the fields and farms. So diverse is the population, and so attuned is the native population to the Bible and Christianity that all are treated equal so that the vote is given to all residents, regardless of race or wealth. Of particular interest to me is Mumu explaining the concept of private property that has just been approved by the government. Where the king once owned all, now a man can buy and covet his own land.

It makes me wonder how far my savings would take me toward the purchase of a farm? The rainfall is plentiful, the soils deep and rich. Something to think on. Looking at the lush mountainsides we're sailing by, I'd guess it would be hard to keep things from growing.

By midnight I consider myself decently versed and ready to present the king or his cohorts with the captain's regards and a case of fine French brandy.

## 25

We are forced to moor the ship a hundred yards from the piers, as nine whaling vessels occupy the harbor and all off-loading facilities. We are rowed ashore and instructed to hire a jolly boat for our return if the ship had yet to find itself dockside.

Whalers are not renowned for the beauty of their vessels, usually stinking to high heaven as they render whale oil, smoke roiling up through their rigging, coating all with black slime. And the hands, sailors, are little better. The ships in the harbor maintain that reputation, although it is a harbor rule to keep their fires contained and refrain from the rendering process while in port.

Our destination is Hale Ali'i, which Mumu informs me is translated as House of the Chiefs. It's a short hike and I'm impressed with the modern buildings in what I'd been led to believe is a savage land. Sailors exaggerate. Not surprisingly the largest building is a brick chandlery, providing all sorts of fittings and line, clothing, and even foodstuffs to supply the many ships.

The capitol building itself is a handsome structure, wood, whitewashed, with a wide covered porch totally surrounding and grounds covered with majestic monkeypod and banyan trees, one of which is at least ten feet in diameter. Alongside the structure are shrubs covered with brilliant yellow blooms, *mamani* it's called, Mumu tells me as we mount the dozen steps leading to a carved door of some local hardwood. As I see no joints the tree that birthed that door had to be at least six feet in diameter. Comfortable lounge chairs cover the porch, with side tables which I imagine are often covered with drinks. It's an inviting structure befitting the capital of a tropical country.

We are greeted by a man in native dress, what I'd call a skirt and open-toed sandals. His shirt is white and loose, open at the neck. He's at least as large as Mumu, who, unlike Mumu's almost constant smile, has a serious continence and is all business. He relieves Mumu of his load of the case of brandy, looks us over carefully as if checking for arms, asks us our business, takes the case, and bides us take a seat. He disappears with the case of brandy; I presume to check the contents.

We are not kept waiting long as a small but well-dressed gentlemen strides into the parlor waiting room and extends a hand. Doctor Gerrit Judd, Mumu has instructed me, was formerly a missionary and physician who accepted the job as adviser, minister, translator, and counselor to the king. I have mixed emotions about the distinguished gentleman—in coat, waistcoat, and four-in-hand tie even in the warm day—as I know he renounced his American citizenship to become a Sandwich Islander.

"Welcome," he says to me as he shakes. "*Aloha*," and "*A' ole palikir*," to Mumu, the former I know is hello and goodbye, the latter I don't remember, but remind myself to ask later. Doctor Judd invites us into his office, where he takes a seat behind a beautiful carved desk and invites us to take a cushioned pair of chairs.

"The *Orient* is a trading vessel?" he asks, and I explain our cargo and intent to also trade at Lahaina. He smiles as if he approves.

He explains, "We're in dire need of lumber suitable for building since the council approved private land sales."

As the captain instructed, I offer an apology. "We heard the reports of the French ship and the looting of the city. My captain, Herschel Constantine, offers his apology that our gift is French brandy."

Dr. Judd laughs, then as the captain hopes, extends his invitation. "I'm sure the captain is busy trying to get alongside the wharf, as the king is busy with affairs, but we have a gathering of captains tomorrow evening for supper and a short talk by the king, and please extend our invitation to him. Seven o'clock should he care to join us."

"I'm instructed to accept your invitation on his behalf."

"Thank you," and he stands which I presume is our signal to excuse ourselves. He repeats the "Thank you," and a *"mahalo"* which I know is thank you in the Sandwich Island language. Then he stops us at the door, and addresses me, "Mr. Zane, are you interested in our flora, fauna, and geology?"

"Very much so, sir," I reply.

"And your physical condition?"

I have to smile. "I'm normally the first to the topsail yardarm, sir."

"I don't suppose you'd like to join other Americans

who've been given permission to climb Mauna Kea? It's a rare privilege as the mountain is a holy place to islanders."

"I'm complimented, sir. I'm not a formally educated man, but as self-educated as is possible with limited access to libraries. I'll ask the captain's permission. This climb is scheduled for when?"

"You should meet the others tomorrow and get equipped. It will take a week to accomplish, but I imagine the *Orient* will be here that long?"

"Then a week in Lahaina."

"Be back here this afternoon, or tomorrow evening with the captain should he attend our supper, which Theodore Allenthorpe, the archaeologist and volcanologist who's leading the climb, is attending. He has equipment for his porters, all islanders, so can easily outfit you."

As we return to the ship, I can't help but wonder how much of a task it will be to climb the huge volcano on the Sandwich Island's biggest island, Hawaii. It lays over one hundred miles to the southeast of our current moorage in Honolulu. I know it's a very tall mountain, so tall that even in this tropical clime, only twenty degrees north of the equator, it's normally snow covered. Unless, of course, the volcano is active...and it's one of the most active in the world, or so I've read.

Do I really want to climb a volcano?

## 26

WE PAY A NATIVE A DIME TO ROW US TO THE SHIP IN HIS outrigger canoe, called a *wa'a*. While the *Orient* is still unable to find a spot at the wharf, the crew is busy repairing and refitting with goods hauled from shore chandlery in her jolly boats.

The captain is in his quarters, and I go directly there, leaving Mumu behind as the second mate needed his brawn the instant we boarded. He yells "Enter" before I finish knocking.

"Report," he says without so much as a howdy-do.

"Yes, sir. Case delivered and I've returned with an invitation for you to attend a supper with other ship captains, and others, tomorrow evening at seven."

"Humph," he grunts, then continues, "I'd hoped for a one-on-one with the king, but this will do. Is he an impressive fellow?"

"We met with his counselor, Doctor Gerrit Judd, who was an impressive fellow, dressed befitting a judge, senator, or even president. And polite without a pompous air. He expressed his thanks on behalf of the king for the brandy and laughed when I told him you were sorry it was French."

"Fine, Zane. You did well. Did the sailor, Mumu, return with you?"

"He did."

"I worried he'd jump ship, being among his countrymen."

"There's one other thing, Captain?"

"And that is?"

"Dr. Judd invited me to join an expedition of Americans who have permission...I guess hard to obtain...to climb Mauna Kea, the volcano on the large island."

He eyes me for a long moment, then asks, "Did you ask to join this adventure?"

"No, sir. He brought it up and thought the ship might enjoy the shared glory with other Americans."

That's a slight exaggeration, but I think he'd care little about loaning me out unless there was some gain for the *Orient*. He is a Boston trader, after all. I'm pleased he seems deep in thought for a moment.

"That is interesting," he says.

"I understand you'll meet the expedition's leader at the supper tomorrow night. The gentleman's name is Theodore Allenthorpe."

"Then I'll reserve my decision until after I have a chance to confer with Mr. Allenthorpe."

"Yes, sir."

"You're excused."

I salute and spin on my heel, but he stops me before I reach the door.

"Zane, do you know of the Ex Ex?"

"I read something about the Exploring Expedition, sir. They mapped much of the Pacific islands and discovered Antarctica, although there's some dispute on that.

And they ended up in court-martial court fighting among the officers."

"Yes, a pity, as it was exploration to overshadow even Lewis and Clark. But that's neither here nor there. A dozen years ago or so Wilkes and fifty of his men climbed the volcano, maybe the fourth party to ever do so. Many got terribly sick from the altitude and almost didn't make it back down…the mountain is near fourteen thousand feet. Are you sure this is something you'd like to attempt?"

"I've been near ten thousand feet with little or no effects."

"Ten is not fourteen, young man."

"I'd like to try it, sir. Others are going, and if I'm to be truthful, I feel I'm as good as the next man."

The captain chuckles. "Aww, the confidence of youth. I'll give you my decision tomorrow evening after the supper at the king's." He was silent a moment, then added, "It would be bragging rights to have our ensign atop the highest mountain in the land."

"And I'd be proud to place it there."

"An interesting thought."

"Aye, sir. Thank you, sir."

With some concern I might not be able to return to the ship, if I'm given permission to go on the volcano climbing adventure, I spend my remaining time off packing my goods so I can grab and go if the time comes. And if it does, I'll have to retrieve my weapons from the ship's armory where Captain Constantine has stowed them.

And I hope the time does come.

My next task, following Bosun Owsley's orders, is removing the ricking from cargo the ship hopes to sell in Honolulu, much of it deep in the bowel of the ship's bilge. It's a hot, sweaty, dank, and dirty job but I have Mumu and his muscle to help.

Before the day is out, we've been cleared to pull alongside the wharf and First Mate Lattrell is entrusted to do so as the captain is going ashore to his supper with the king, some of his cabinet, and other captains in port. And I hope a meeting with archaeologist and volcanologist, Theodore Allenthorpe.

I'm happy to be kept busy on the mainmast topgallant crossarm, setting sail to one-quarter is height enough to help with steerageway to dock the big vessel, while both jolly boats, assisted by two hired from ashore, put rowing muscle to work to guide and assist. It's nearly a two-hour process, but soon we're secured next to a pair of overhead cranes capable of off-loading lifts of lumber weighing all of one thousand pounds apiece. Those, and crates of iron goods take us well into the night.

I hope to be called to the captain's quarters before my shift is over, but it's not to be and in anticipation of my, hopeful, forthcoming adventure, toss and turn during my four hours off. Being securely at the dock, I'm sure the captain, who I know has returned, will sleep through the night, but I'm wrong, I'm beckoned to his quarters just after the witching hour.

"Pack," he says. "Allenthorpe's man will meet you at the shore end of the wharf at dawn. You can secure a locker at the chandlery for a small sum to stow belongings you'll not want to carry up the mountain." He rises and walks around the desk and hands me a ship's ensign, the ship flag probably three feet by five feet, along with some fine, quarter-inch line. "Raise this proudly, but well below the flag of the Sandwich Islands or the U.S.A. Understand?"

"Clearly, sir."

"And stay well, young man. It wouldn't do to have you cooked like a sausage in some lava pit."

"Yes, sir. I mean no, sir. I mean it certainly wouldn't do. Thank you, sir."

"If you're not back here in five days and find us at sea, catch an island schooner to Lahaina where we'll likely be anchored for a week. I'll reimburse you the passage."

"Yes, sir. Good trading while here."

"Go get some rest. You'll need it." He laughs as I salute and leave.

Tomorrow, off to the Big Island, a mountain nearly as high as any west of the Mississippi.

And a new challenge.

## 27

I'M SURPRISED TO BE MET BY DR. JUDD AT THE END OF THE wharf, who introduces me to his companion, George Bernheim, a horticulturist.

"I'll need to hire a locker to stow the goods I'm not wanting to carry," I say to both.

"The *Wanderer* has room for your goods," George advises, and picks up one of my two bundles. "She'll lay over while we're on the mountain."

I'd noticed the schooner *Wanderer* moored far out in the harbor and admired the beautiful boat, eighty feet I'd guess. She is to be our transportation to Hilo, on the north side of the Big Island, a two-hundred-twenty-five-mile sail. From there it's twenty-five miles or so and nearly a fourteen-thousand-foot climb to the edge of the smoking volcano.

We stride a quarter mile around the harbor front to where a half-dozen men are gathered, loading a twenty-foot shore boat with what seems to be their personal goods. I am quickly introduced and eight of us load up and four of us grab oars to head to the *Wanderer*. I give

Dr. Judd a wave and receive one in return. Allenthorpe is not among us, so I presume he is already aboard. And he is, he greets us as we board and leads us to quarters below, which in our case is hammocks on the ship's single cargo deck. As we stow our belongings, I hear the anchor chains rattling into the chain lockers both forward and aft. We waste no time getting underway.

Allenthorpe immediately calls a meeting as we clear the harbor, heading into a golden eastern sky as we head into a rising sun. A stiff breeze has the sails taut and the crew is setting staysails to take full advantage of the wind off our aft quarter. As we leave Honolulu behind, I bet we're making fourteen knots, nicely heeled to our portside. We gather on the main deck to hear what the expedition leader has to say.

"Gentlemen, I plan to make this climb in two and a half days, spend a day atop the mountain, making observations, then descend in less than forty-eight hours. We'll be met at Hilo by forty native porters, Kanakas, who will carry our gear and instruments. Should you, Mr. Bernheim, or you, Mr. Quinton, want to stop and collect specimens, that's up to you as we'll charge on and you may follow. I'd suggest you not let us out of sight as the underbrush is thick, in fact impassable in places. Now, get some nourishment, the cook is at your service, and some rest. The challenge of our lifetime is just ahead. God protect us all."

I learn that Quinton, is Horace Quinton, who's the expedition's zoologist and botanist, and his scientific expertise must be highly desired as he appears to be a man who'd have trouble climbing the ladder to board the *Wanderer*, much less the mountain. He's at least eight inches shorter than my six feet and must weigh near twice my one hundred eighty pounds. He's one of those folks, I notice, that when we head for the ladder to descend to the main deck and the four tables just outside the cook's door, he sort of leans forward to begin his trek, and accelerates until he finds something to grab to stop his progress. Then he has to squeeze through the passageway. I'll bet this man doesn't make one thousand of the nearly fourteen thousand feet.

While filling our bellies with salt fish and yams, fresh from Honolulu, I am seated next to the expedition's geologist, Orval McBean, a graying-at-the-temples gentleman more than twice my age, but unlike Mr. Quinton seems in fine physical condition.

"And where did you study your trade, if I may ask?" I inquire.

"You may. Williams College, Williamstown, Massachusetts. One of the world's finest. Very difficult to gain acceptance. I studied under the prestigious Ebenezer Emmons. I'm a member of the American Association of Geologists and am proud to be the first with my superior education to ascend and study this mountain."

McBean has an air of superiority about him, great disdain for others, and seems to talk down his nose at me. He almost sneers as he asks, "And where did you study, young man?"

"Zanes," I say, with some confidence. "A portable university from St. Joe, Missouri, to Oregon."

"I beg your pardon?" he asks with a deep frown, seeming perplexed.

"My parents were fine teachers, as was the task of getting prepared for and navigating the Oregon Trail, then back trails to San Francisco. I learned mechanics and physics and engineering transporting heavy wagons up and down cliffs and across streams. I learned military battle tactics on the go with Indian adversaries both day and night, and close combat with a few rotten white men. I learned medicine, treating and helping doctor cholera, broken bones, arrow and gunshot wounds. I even learned some of your trade, geology, while hunting water holes and natural landmarks. Not to speak of biology and zoology, learning what critters to follow to obtain water, their tracks and scat, and how to track and kill for meat. I even became a fair cook. I guess you could say my university was, and still is, a life lesson."

Others at the table had quieted as I spoke and broke into laughter as I finished and all McBean had to say was an "Humph," and he turned away to talk to the gentleman on his other side. I believe he reddened, blushed, but it was hard to tell as he'd given me his back. I realize I was being a little offensive, not seeming to value his high-priced education, but he was arrogant, and arrogance offends me. So, I quietly lashed out and seem to have gained favor with others at the table.

All that said I hope to learn a lot from the educated men on this expedition, and possibly even teach them some practical knowledge learned on the trail.

We are each issued a thick canvas backpack and there's a selection of thick-soled brogans to choose from. My own are city shoes and I imagine my canvas made for me by Mumu will not stand up to sharp shards of volcanic rock. Leather gloves are provided for those who wish and having seen the snow atop the mountain when earlier passed, I take advantage. I'm thinking both for the cold and for the sharp lava.

Mauna Kea will be an unforgiving slope to navigate offering the insult of heat, razor-sharp shards, the possibility of breaking through a thin surface, and poisonous gas that can kill, if what I've read of volcanoes is true.

We spend the rest of the day with a steady wind,

organizing personal gear, reading, and relaxing. Supper is more yams and the treat of fresh ham, then we retire to deck and enjoy the crew singing chanteys, and one of my particular favorites I learned aboard the *Windsong*, "Heave Away":

> *"Come get your duds in order*
> *For we're going to leave tomorrow,*
> *Heave away, me jollies, heave away.*
> *Come get your duds in order*
> *For we're going to cross the water,*
> *Heave away me jolly boys, we're all bound away."*

> *"Sometimes we're bound for Liverpool,*
> *Sometimes we're bound for Spain,*
> *But now we're bound for Hilo town*
> *To watch the girls a-dancing."*

> *"Now it's farewell Maggie darling,*
> *For it's now I'm going to leave you,*
> *You promised me you'd marry me,*
> *But how you did deceive me."*
> *"I wrote me love a letter*
> *And I signed it with a ring,*
> *I wrote me love a letter,*
> *I was on the Jenny Lind."*
> *"Sometimes we're bound for Liverpool,*
> *Sometimes we're bound for Spain,*
> *But now we're bound for Hilo town*
> *To watch the girls a-dancing."*

I'm no skilled tenor but I sing along. I know the song so know they substituted Hilo town for St. John's town and miss voicing the change in the first verse but not the second. No matter as the tune is no less catchy.

I'm to my hammock before the rest of them, for tomorrow will be a test of will and endurance.

I do think of Nancy Ann Tannenbaum as I know we'll pass Lahaina in the night near dawn. I hope she's well, and to be truthful, hope she's thinking of me.

## 28

We've been nineteen hours at sea as we drop the hooks off Hilo. From here the mountain looks like an easy hike—nice, rounded slopes to the skyline. But it's a foolish man who looks at the skyline not knowing what lies beyond and makes any presumptions. Many a time from St. Joe to Oregon I eyed a pleasant skyline only to top it and see hard-shouldered mountains ahead and the skyline merely a hump in the landscape hiding what lay beyond. The top of the mountain is just fifteen degrees south of due west, if the map is correct, and the setting sun is already below the mountain. We'll not see the glory of sunset or the fiery globe dropping below the skyline, but the backlit mountain does give up the fact it's tree and brush covered at least as high as we can visualize.

Allenthorpe has ordered us all ashore, sending crewmen ahead to set up four-man tents that will accompany us on our journey. I retrieve two of my four weapons from the captain. My shotgun will fit nicely in my pack when broken in half, and my Navy Colt on its belt. Powder horn, balls, and buckshot will ride in my pack. I've said nothing to Allenthorpe or anyone about bringing the scattergun, but it's handy for critters should the need arise—both edible and two-footed ones.

We go in shifts the two hundred yards ashore, six men to a jolly boat leaving one to row back to the ship. With only two boats, it's four trips for each as gear has to be hauled. It's after eight at night by the time we're settled in our tent camp and rather than cook the evening meal, Allenthorpe has arranged for the small town's only hotel to feed us, the usual yams, only this time with slow cooked sowbelly and the local concoction of what they call poi. A bland mush but filling, which made me wish for molasses. We are treated with fresh mangos and cane sugar that serves handily as dessert.

A few of the men stay up around the campfire singing to a mouth harp, or harmonica as it's come to be called, which is fine with me as they sing me to sleep with only one other man already sawing logs in our tent.

I'm awakened thinking the wind must have come up and blown a tree down on me, then whatever it is outside the tent but squished down on me, yells some profanities and scrambles off, and I'm able to get to my feet. All hell has broken loose outside, and I manage to pull my trousers on and exit the tent flap, only to have to step back inside as a man careens past, his arms windmilling, and he goes to his back.

Four are involved in the brawl, a drunken brawl I soon surmise as far more blows are thrown than land. Almost as quickly as it's started it's broken up by Allenthorpe, in his nightshirt. I'm not particularly surprised to see one of the combatants, now bleeding from a gashed eyebrow and his nose, is the arrogant McBean, the geologist. I guess he looked down his long, highly educated, proboscis at the wrong commoner. I can't help but be a little amused.

As soon as Allenthorpe and his helpers have the four men at bay, he snaps, so angry he's spitting with every word, "All right you worthless scoundrels, who brought the whiskey?"

One of the men, a flat-faced, balding fellow with little Irish ears, bleeding from his nose, wipes the blood away with the back of his hand and answers. "Bought it from a Kanaka," he mumbles.

I can't help but think of one of my father's favorite sayings, "If it weren't for whiskey, the Irish would rule the world."

Allenthorpe takes a deep breath and keeps his voice even, but commanding, "All of you, listen up. There will be no drunkenness…no, no alcohol, period, on this venture. I'm the captain of this voyage, even be it a land voyage, and the next man caught with alcohol will be given ten lashes. And the next man who throws a blow in anger will be given twenty. Do you understand?"

He gets a general acquiescence from the men, most of who are now gathered in a circle around him.

"Any man doesn't like it can stay and look for work in Hilo or stoking the fires on some filthy whaling vessel." Then he adds, "Do any of you need medical assistance?"

Getting no response, he commands, "Now, you four who were fighting put that tent back right and all of you get to your bedrolls, get to sleep. We'll be up at four o'clock and on the mountain by six."

And he's a man of his word. I'm poked awake at four in the morning, and we've tied down our backpacks and rolled up the tent, rope, and stakes in ten minutes. We breakfast by firelight with hardtack, mango, coconut milk laced with rare chocolate, and coffee.

It's a good thing we have the forty Kanaka porters, as there are cases of instruments to carry in addition to a week's supply of foodstuff and two hundred gallons of water, which surprises me a little. I'd think with a tropical clime low down and snow above, water would be little problem. But it seems Allenthorpe has done his studies on climbing this volcano. Luckily, I'm tasked with only carrying my personal goods. We all have, or soon acquire, walking sticks along the way.

We are quite a procession as we set out. Two Kanaka guides lead, with Allenthorpe and Bernheim, his horticulturist next; then the arrogant Orval McBean, geologist; with the obese zoologist, botanist and biologist, Horace Quinton, close behind. Then I'm instructed to follow him closely. A pity as I can barely see the country ahead as Quinton is an ax handle wide. I'm followed by more than a dozen of Allenthorpe's crew—the cook, a pair of Kanakas carrying Allenthorpe's small folding writing desk and personal items, a pair of armed expedition guards carrying both rifles and sidearms, and others whose duties I know not. They carry only their backpacks. None of the others seem armed.

I soon discover I can also barely hear the birds and breaking of brush over Quinton's wheezing, huffing, and puffing. Being a hunter, often living off the land, I learned to travel as silently as possible. After the first three hundred yards and fifty feet of elevation behind us, Quinton stops and turns. He's already red-faced and wheezing.

"Young Zane, please locate my canteen. I'm afraid it's deep in my pack."

As I have my own in a satchel, along with a half-dozen palms full of macadamia nuts, firmly affixed to my belt, I offer it. I don't want to fall behind. "Sir, be my guest as mine's at hand."

"Aw, sir, you play the fine gentleman. I pray it's true the total trip." He takes two deep draws on my water, emptying at least a third of it.

"It will be a long trip," I caution as I replace my canteen.

"My endurance will surprise you, young Zane," he says with some finality and resumes his climb, now twenty-five paces behind those leading. I'm not convinced.

"Allenthorpe says we'll make near halfway before nightfall," I say with some caution obvious.

He ignores me, seemingly concentrating, not on the trail, but on the surroundings.

I notice Quinton has a short-bladed knife, a skinning configuration, in hand, and soon learn why. He occasionally clips the end of branches as we pass, stuffing them into an eighteen-inch-long sack hanging from his belt. He has a small notebook and draws and takes notes as he walks. I guess he's a botanist on the prowl.

I can't help but wonder what a strain on his already overworked heart this constant climb must be. Then, after no more than a mile, he proves it as he stops, and plops down.

"I have to rest, young Zane. Can I trouble you to stay with me?"

I sigh deeply then ask, "Hold on. I'll get Allenthorpe's permission."

"Must you?" he calls after me.

"Yes, sir, he is expedition leader," I call back over my shoulder, and continue on.

## 29

"I THINK NOT," ALLENTHORPE SAYS, AND I'M PLEASED HE does. "I gave my word to Captain Constantine that you'd make the top if I did, and that you'd fare well. I'll leave a Kanaka with him. I feared something like this. Thank God we're not halfway up the mountain. He can easily return from here. There are plants and critters galore within a hundred yards from town, so he'll have his eye glued to a magnifying glass until we return. He's my uncle on my mother's side, or I'd never have permitted him along."

I'm a little surprised that Constantine was concerned about my welfare. I smile. "Do you want me to pick the most roly-poly of the Kanakas?"

He chuckles. "A wise idea, Master Zane. When you have him settled, catch up and climb with me."

"Yes, sir, my pleasure," I reply, then hurry away to finish my assignment. He must think me a little younger than my majority of eighteen, as it's normally a time to stop calling a young man master rather than mister. Should he do so again pride will demand I correct him.

I spot a well-rounded Kanaka with a fairly small load, yell to the others for an English speaker, and a tall muscular fellow steps out and I instruct him to take the man's smallish pack and divide it among the others, then to instruct him to stay, care for, and obey Mr. Quinton. He does so then turns to me.

"I stay with you, English," he says and it's not a request.

"And you are?"

"Koa," he replies, and slaps his chest, obviously proud of his name.

"American, not English. But fine, stay with me, but slightly behind as I'm joining the expedition *moi*." Mumu has taught me the Hawaiian name for king, *moi*.

He nods, and we're off to catch up with Allenthorpe.

"I'd prefer you!" Quinton calls out as we stride away.

"Sorry, Allenthorpe's orders," I call back over my shoulder.

We catch up and I offer, "Done, sir."

"You've acquired an admirer?" Allenthorpe says, eyeing Koa, seemingly amused.

"A helper at least. This is Koa," I introduce them and Allenthorpe nods. "He speaks English."

"Onward, upward," Allenthorpe says, and continues to climb.

As it's arduous work, we move on silently, saving our breath for the climb. When the sun is high overhead we cross the crown we can see below, and the hulk of the mountain towers before us. We see the enormity of our next effort. When we reach a slight plateau, Allenthorpe calls for lunch and a rest and we all drop packs and flop down and dig into our packs for packets, paper wrapped that were passed among us before sunlight this morning.

Unwrapping I discover small fruits and nuts, hardtack, and a few ounces of salt pork.

Koa is beside me and when we finish, he asks. "You American? What island?"

That makes me smile. "America is a giant land of states and territories, not islands. I am now from Oregon, recently from California, but going back to Oregon soon."

"I know of San Francisco. Work on fur ship brig *Polar Wind.* Learn English tongue there."

"You learned well."

"No like, kill too many seal and otter. Not go back."

"But made money?"

He nods. "Make lots money. Give to Mama."

Again, I smile. "A dutiful son. I also send money to Mama and sisters."

He nods, and smiles.

I continue, "Did you reach the ice country of Alaska?"

"Two months in Alaska. Like here, ice on mountaintop. Many trees, many seal and otter."

"You were there in the summer, I guess. In winter, ice and snow everywhere if what I read is correct."

He shrugs his big shoulders.

Allenthorpe yells us all to our feet and we're off again.

We only climb a mile before we face a solid wall of head-high shrubs, thick as hair on a hog, and even our leading guides who carry machetes can't begin to clear a path.

Allenthorpe seems nonplussed and begins to side the hill. And in less than a mile we come to a well-aged lava flow, now hard as the hubs of hell, and we get our first real taste of razor-sharp shards of what was once smooth, but now shattered with small ravines having to be leaped, and sharp edges avoided.

Looking behind at those following I get apprehensive for the first time. The Kanakas, carrying the lion's share of our supplies, are complaining among themselves, and I must express my doubts to Allenthorpe.

I move up alongside him. "Sir, I'll be surprised if our natives stay the course."

"I noticed," he says, not breaking stride. "Send your man, Koa, back among them when we camp and ask him to judge their intent."

"Yes, sir," I say, deciding to wait until the campsite to address my new friend.

Another five hours of climbing again mostly off the lava flow and on more easily crossed soil and greenery, and Allenthorpe selects a gentler slope for camp.

I notice a flight of what appear to be geese, winging low overhead and disappearing off a small rise to the east of us.

As Allenthorpe is directing the erection of his tent, I wander over.

"Sir, did you notice the geese?"

"Nene, they are called here."

"May I try and harvest a few for supper?"

"Hard to hit with that Colt?"

"Have my shotgun in my pack."

He looks a little serious for a moment as if he doesn't approve, then I think he has visions of roast goose and relents. I quickly assemble my shotgun, putting a half-dozen extra shells in my pocket.

And we're off to hunt.

## 30

As I suspected, when Koa and I crest the near rise a two-hundred-pace-long by fifty-pace-wide pond appears not a hundred feet below. The shrub surrounding is nearly as thick as that we'd confronted below, so it's easy to put the sneak on them. There are at least three hundred nene covering the pond, dipping long necks to feed on bottom greenery. They are beautiful birds, not quite so large as our Canada geese, but proportioned the same. Their nearly coal-black heads are striking against gray stripes down wings, neck, and across back, with gray breasts.

Silently I instruct Koa to circle the pond and then cause a ruckus to cause them to fly my way and in a few minutes he does so as I do a belly crawl to get within a dozen yards of the edge of the pond.

I hear him yell and the pond explodes with wingbeats. I fire a little too quickly and two birds fall before clearing the pond. Others circle and Koa jumps up and down, yelling and causing them to reverse direction and come back my way. They have to work to gain elevation as the steep mountain is at my back. So, slowing they're an easy shot. Two more shots, and two more fall, these, thankfully, into the brush. By the time I'm able to reload, the fast-flying flock is well beyond range.

Koa dives in the pond and swims like a seal to retrieve the birds. We gather our harvest and head back, only to see all the Kanakas gathered around Allenthorpe's tent, and they don't seem happy.

Voices raised, shaking fists...not a good sign.

Even the two guides, machetes in hand, have taken the side of the others. Thirty-nine Kanakas stand, facing Allenthorpe and twenty-three Anglos, standing with hands on hips, sour looks, and furrowed brows.

"Koa, please discover what the problem is," I say. He moves among the Kanakas as I sidle up next to Allenthorpe. My shotgun, reloaded, still in hand, seems to quiet the natives as Koa speaks to those seeming to lead this small rebellion. He quiets them, then comes to face us.

"Lava has cut up their sandals, some feet bleed. They say they go no more."

"I need four to carry instruments onward." He turns to George Bernheim, "We're about to the tree line. There will be no more foliage for you to study when we're four or five hundred feet higher. You stay and command this camp. Give up your boots."

"My boots? Hell no. Then my feet—"

Allenthorpe stops him cold. "Bernheim, give up your boots." Then he points to another of his expedition members. "You, too, Josephson. Boots, now. We'll trade the Kanakas for sandals. You'll get them back." Then back to Koa. "Four men, double pay, make four others give up their sandals. So two of the men will have boots, two will have two extra pair of sandals."

"What pay for sandals," Koa asks.

"Two American dollars the pair," Allenthorpe answers quickly and Koa nods.

And we climb on, Allenthorpe and the two guides in the lead; McBean, the arrogant geologist following; Koa and myself, are just ahead of the two Kanakas with extra sandals.

Eight of us to make what appears to be the final four thousand feet. As we are at or near ten thousand, the air is noticeably thinner and we've slowed our pace. We pass what Allenthorpe and McBean describe as a vent, a ten-foot diameter hole that occasionally belches smoke and a nauseous gas which drives us away to circle it from more than fifty yards. After another thousand feet of hard climbing, we're surprised by a sudden cutting, cold wind and within minutes snow, blowing horizontally. All of us were cautioned to bring slickers and they're quickly donned. But the frigid wind cuts right through them, even though they're supposed to be rain and windproof.

The wind increases to gale force and Allenthorpe orders the Kanakas to put up the two tents which is their primary load, but it's fruitless. We'd retreat, but into the wind and blowing snow it would be a fool's errand.

And attempting to erect the tents is equally frustrating.

"Roll up," Allenthorpe commands, "and we'll ride it out."

With four to a tent, we enclose ourselves in canvas, and the tent canvas becomes our cocoons, and as we lay side to side to capture whatever body heat we can from our neighbor, the wind whips and howls and the snow piles upon us.

Hour after hour we hunker down. I have to wonder how ironic it would be, a sail into the warm South

Pacific climes becomes a frozen grave high on an over one-thousand-degree-plus lava-pregnant mountain. Probably a grave never to be found.

That said, I learned on my trip across the country on the Oregon Trail, a snow cave will keep a man alive, and four men more easily so. Water freezes and becomes ice and snow at thirty-two degrees, and the blowing snow and frigid air outside our blanket of snow can become much colder and far more life-threatening. So Allenthorpe has made another wise decision.

Like moles, we stick our heads up out of our snow hole when the sound of the wind aborts. To our shock the sun is up over the imaginary yardarm and clear, glistening off the snow as if the mountain was carpeted with diamonds.

It's still cold and only then do I realize how cold the Kanakas much be, in sandals and their skirt-like native dress. As Allenthorpe gathers us together after we dig out and roll our tents, I'm not surprised when the natives, all but Koa, refuse to go on. We are all light-headed and two of the Kanakas have thrown up, which Allenthorpe attributes to altitude sickness. We're still three thousand feet below the rim of the caldera, the bowl that is the volcano itself.

Strangely enough water is our primary problem, although there is at least a two-foot depth of the frozen version all around us. We empty our packs of personal items so they'll hold one of the large gourds, maybe as much as a gallon, of water. Leaving those personal items with the four remaining Kanakas who are instructed to remain with the tents as well.

So, it's Allenthorpe, Koa, McBean, and I who, with now very deliberate steps, place foot after foot as it's as steep as climbing a stairway. For nearly a thousand feet, it's very difficult as we change the lead often to break a pathway in the snow, but soon I realize it's melted off due to ground heat. The first real indication it's an active volcano beneath our feet.

And I wonder, how hot will it get?

## 31

Now there's not a wisp of a living thing on the mountain. It's just as well Bernheim, the horticulturist, was ordered to stay below. Only the volcanologist and geologist have subjects to study. It's also just as well we left the instruments behind as I'd guess no one will have the energy to utilize them for whatever experiments they're intended.

As we climb, now it's find a comfortable outcropping and rest every hundred steps or so. When only five hundred feet or so from what appears to be the top, McBean collapses, then stands almost immediately, rubbing his backside as if it's covered with ants.

Looking bewildered, he mumbles. "Rock's too hot… but I must go no farther. Terrible headache."

"You'll…miss…the caldera," Allenthorpe says. His speech is broken with a breath almost between each word.

I have a headache as well, and am slightly nauseous, but the excitement of seeing inside a volcano, of planting the ship's ensign, drives me on. After another five hundred feet or so, leaving McBean resting on his folded slicker atop a rock, even Koa craters. He has a hand on each knee and is throwing up.

Allenthorpe studies him a moment. "No need for lunch as we'll likely give it back to the mountain."

I lay a hand on Koa's broad shoulder. "Move back down the mountain and join the others." And he nods his agreement.

He mumbles, "God's place here. Not ours."

I nod, not totally sure he's not correct. Then I turn to Allenthorpe. "Let's get there, place our flags," I mumble, "and get back down. My feet are burning up."

"And mine," Allenthorpe parrots.

Koa retreats and we charge on, if you can call very deliberate steps charging. We continually have to wipe the sweat away.

To our surprise, when we crest the edge we can see from below, the top appears flat, jagged but flat with the occasional uplift table rock, for a hundred paces to the edge of the caldera itself. But as we move forward, we come across a giant fissure, twenty feet across, the depth of which cannot be judged as fifty feet below it's smoke-filled. It looks to be the hot, gaseous, entrance to hell. We move to the side fifty paces until we can circumvent the smoking obstacle. We have to do so again at another fissure equally foreboding before the great chasm—a bowl over a mile across—opens before us. There is no descending, not that I'd want to, as a sheer cliff of over one hundred feet in height rings the caldera. Only one pool of molten lava appears, and it's more than halfway across the wile wide bowl. Several other spots are smoking, and one, thankfully almost to the far edge, spits fire and balls of molten lava over one hundred feet above its surface.

"Not...too...close," Allenthorpe cautions as we near the edge. Now it's so hot I have to glance down occasionally to make sure my boots are not afire, in fact the souls are smoking and seeming to stick to the rock below.

"I...I need no warning," I say, happy to stay fifty feet from where the surface disappears from view. My burning feet attest to how uninviting the place is. And the sweat literally rolling off my brow, now into my eyes, interfering with my vision. I wish I had a neckerchief, but my sleeves have to do. Already wet through, I fear all I'm doing is smearing perspiration.

"Let's...plant our...flags," he says, and moves farther back. Neither of us thought to bring a pole, so we move to a fifteen-foot-high cliff face, one of the many table rocks, with a foot-wide ledge eight feet or so above us, and he suspends both the island flag and that of the U.S.A., careful to keep the latter a foot lower. Then I place our ship's ensign. As we can't actually hang the flags on pegs, even if we had them, we place loose lava stones weighing down the upper seams. As the edge angles downward, this is easy to accomplish, but the flags are cattywampus, one upper corner lower than the other. It's not the best job of work I've ever accomplished. I will make a drawing of this when I return to the ship for the captain and crew's edification. By the time that occurs, I'm sure the wind, and possibly exploding lava rocks, will have rendered all three flags to shreds or even ash.

My vision of high-flying flags waving proudly above the highest mountain in the Sandwich Islands is dashed about as quickly as we dash away from the edge of that totally foreign environment.

I'm sucking deep breaths as we descend and realize I

can't get the stench of whatever god-awful gasses are being belched from the caldera out of my nose. I hope it's not a permanent condition and that the hot air has not scalded my nose, throat, or lungs, but it seems to lessen as we descend farther. When we reach the snow line, I'm happy to rub now slightly melting wet snow over my arms, face, and the back of my neck. Snow that was such a short time ago a deadly enemy is now a welcome friend. And it's wet enough to give thirst some relief.

To our surprise we have to stop and rest as often on the descent as we did on the ascent, and not to my surprise do we find our personal goods and tents in a pile where we'd left them. With no McBean or Kanakas in sight. Truthfully, I have no ill feelings toward them as I think a retreat was wise. We abandon the heavy tents, gather up our personals, leave the water gourds, now empty, and head lower with purpose.

The descent is much easier than the ascent, not only because it's downhill but because the path through the snow is stomped down and our path clear.

When three or four hundred feet below the snow line, Koa and McBean await, and after another thousand feet, the balance of our crew and Kanakas are assembled in a comfortable camp.

They want to continue on, but we are totally exhausted. I believe our condition is not so much from the climb as from breathing the foul air, and maybe from worry about our very existence, which can be a debilitating condition. Allenthorpe and I follow the setting sun to slumber, ignoring supper.

We make up for it at breakfast, eating a full bowl the mush they call poi, macadamia nuts, all lathered in molasses, and a whole mango each.

Reaching the edge of a five-mile descent to Hilo, I'm surprised to make out a full three-masted ship in the harbor. It looks remarkably like the *Orient,* which is supposed to be at the wharf in Lahaina.

Am I to miss what I hoped would be an assignation with beautiful Nancy Ann Tannenbaum?

## 32

WE ARRIVE IN HILO IN LESS THAN TWO HOURS, WITH ONLY a half hour of daylight left, following a fairly well-trod path through the jungle-like foliage. The ship is, in fact, the *Orient*. But that's not my only worried observation. A crowd of locals, maybe two hundred strong, is gathered on the edge of the village, facing us as we clear the trees and undergrowth.

At first I think we have a welcoming party who'll greet us with cheers for our accomplishments, then when less than a hundred yards separate us, realize those yells are in anger, not welcome. Then the crowd, with machetes and clubs carved for battle, begin screaming and running our way. Our Kanakas break and scatter back into the forest and Allenthorpe yells to me as he spins on his heel. "Retreat, retreat!"

He must have been a military man in some distant past. No matter, I need little expert encouragement. Even with the Colt on my hip, the shotgun in my pack, and my new friend Koa at my side, I have no interest in attempting to face down a couple of hundred angry natives. Kanakas whose complaints, like their language, I don't understand. I quickly decide I don't want to wait for Koa to interpret their intentions. Screams from a lot of very large, very angry, weapon-wielding men, speak reams.

We run like hell.

I can't help but remember a quote from a book I borrowed from the Lewiston postmaster. A very old book, *The Art of War* by some Chinese general from centuries ago. The quote is "He will win when he knows when to fight and when not to fight." This is clearly a "when not to fight" situation.

Running uphill after hiking over six thousand feet down a steep mountain is no easy task, particularly with a fairly heavy pack on your back. Still, I'm able to keep up with Koa—fear is an excellent fuel—who I'm surprised elected to join us rather than turn around and shake his fist and scream at us.

Allenthorpe yells over his shoulder, "Split up, split up!" And I think he's showing his military acumen again. I wonder if he's read *The Art of War*. Only having fifty or so natives on your tail, if they split up to follow, is likely better than two hundred.

That said, I'm not leaving Koa's tail and follow him closely, being a hinderance at times by holding onto his pack to broach ledges or break through thick greenery. When we reach a particularly thick area of vines and shrubs with leaves the size of elephant ears, he drags me to one side, drops deep into and under foliage, and orders silence.

His ploy works as we hear a long line of Kanakas slushing through the thick jungle, not forty feet from us, on the same game trail we'd snuck from.

We stay silent for several minutes as the crowd of pursuers disappear up the mountain side.

I whisper to Koa, "What did we do?"

"Gods only on mountain. No man."

"But we had permission."

"Not from gods. King powerful, but not all Kanaka care."

Had we not been in such serious condition I'd have chuckled at that. The fact is I don't know their god so who am I to ask his permission, and I doubt Allenthorpe does.

As we talk, I check the loads in my Colt, then assemble and load my scattergun.

Firearms checked, I ask, "What now?"

"*Makai*…Down to sea, take *wa'a* to ship where safe."

"Let's go while they are hunting up the mountain."

Koa moves out, away from the trail we'd traveled, moving west, working through the vines and undergrowth, but always down. *Makai*, he tells me and explains, down to the sea. It's only a few minutes until we break out of the undergrowth onto some rugged rocks bordering the sea on the very east side of the harbor with both the *Orient* and the *Wanderer* moored only a couple of hundred yards away. I breathe easy for the first time since starting the climb.

Luckily a *wahini*, an islander woman, is paddling a *wa'a*, an outrigger, just beyond the low surf. Maybe it's my luck Koa is such a handsome specimen of manhood, as she wastes no time working her way through a couple of rock outcroppings as he wades out to capture her bowline. He waves me out and I only have to get wet up to my thighs and find myself seated between Koa, who's forward, and the *wahini* who's aft with the paddle. She's old, with wrinkles to match a walnut, and twice what was once her girlish weight, but she's full of admiration for Koa as they trade smiles and coy looks. It's a wise man who admires the charms of a helper.

"The big ship," I direct them, and soon find myself climbing a rope ladder to the deck of the *Orient*. Captain Constantine greets me as I leap the taffrail.

"Welcome home," he says, then asks, "What was all the ruckus?"

"Seems some of the locals took umbrage to us climbing their holy mountain."

"Did you make it atop?" he asks, his brows furrowed in doubt.

"We did. I'll draw you a picture when settled. Worst experience of my life. However, the *Orient* ensign is flying high and proud."

"Allenthorpe and his crew?"

"No idea, they ran one way, my friend Koa here and I another. I'd likely be chopped into mackerel bait wasn't for Koa."

Constantine studies the big Kanaka who's followed me onboard, and gives him a nod.

I continue. "He's a seaman, worked a fur seal boat all the way to Alaska. He's likely not welcome back on the island. Can we sign him on?"

"If he wishes to sign aboard as a common seaman, yes. We had two men jump ship in Honolulu. Damn women there are too pretty and way too willing."

Koa asks, "You pay?"

"Seaman's wages."

"I work."

"Are we headed for Lahaina?" I ask.

"No trade goods there, another trader cleaned them out. We're weighing anchor with the tide in two hours.

Wind and the good Lord favor we'll pass the Farallons in nineteen days."

I'm disappointed, but don't say so. "My same cabin?"

"You're with Owsley. You look like hell, grab a bowl if your gut is empty, a cup of grog if it needs calming." I nod, thankful for being aboard a friend ship. The captain continues. "Then take a dogwatch. We'll roll you out in six."

"How about Allenthorpe and his men?"

"They were on their own when we met them. They are under the protection of the king."

"The king's in Honolulu," I say, questioning.

"My responsibility is to the *Orient* and her crew. And it is so for you as well."

I nod, then after a deep breath, acknowledge his comment which is more an order than a comment. "Yes, sir. The *Orient* and her crew. My family at sea."

"A wise observation. Get some rest, young Jake. When you awaken even this huge mountain will be out of sight."

And, so will Nancy Ann Tannenbaum, I think, but don't say.

## 33

IT'S MIDNIGHT WHEN MY DOGWATCH IS OVER AND, PRETTY well rested, I hit the main deck to see Koa and Mumu in conversation. I'm only a little taken aback when Mumu throws his thick arms around me a gives me a squeeze that takes my air away and worries me he'll snap a rib, but he releases me and holds me at arm's length, looking me up and down.

"You okey dokey, young Jake?" he asks.

"Yes...my...friend," I answer, catching my breath. Then add, "You have met my friend, Koa, I see."

"Koa is from my island. Know all my life." And Koa nods and grins wider than I've seen him do since I realized he could speak the English language.

As I'm ordered to the mizzenmast I yell back over my shoulder, "Take care of each other...and me...you are my fine friends."

Koa calls after me, "You know *ohana*?"

I stop and turn back. "No, sir, I do not."

"It mean family, not just Mama and Papa, but all who

are part of you. You are now *ohana* to Mumu and Koa. Family."

"Thank you. I am honored. Family is the most important thing in life. You can depend on me, as I have on you."

I get a smile and wave from both of them, and find myself, in the canvas shoes Mumu made for me, going up the ratlines to the top yardarm to set a staysail. After the mountain, the masts don't seem so high. But I still find myself short of beath. The aftereffects of altitude sickness, I suppose.

First Mate Lattrell strides up, I'm actually happy to see his ugly face, and yells, "Get to it, soggers," but before I can move he slaps me on the back. "Glad you're back safe."

I'm beginning to think I've shed the title of Jack Nastyface.

I quickly find I'm positioned on the yardarm between the fiddle player, Charley O'Donnell, and my old friend Boston Bob. Bob almost immediately asks, "You've climbed the mountain high, with air so thin it be hard to even sigh!"

I laugh, then the smile turns sour as the fiddle player has to add, "Aye, while the captain's pet monkey played on the mountain, the rest of us worked."

He still has a mouth as big as his fiddle. So, I yell back, "I see you're healed up. So, another dance on the deck box is your plan?"

I guess my challenge is answered as he turns away and goes to work, ignoring my suggestion. I'm surprised as I thought we'd become friends, or at least respectful shipmates. But some men require a good thrashing to learn an iota of humility. Charley O'Donnell seems to be one. Happy to oblige him again I won't be so kind without passengers watching.

That evening, before our supper, I'm summoned to the captain's quarters to dine privately with him. I carefully relate the details of the climb and he produces a bit of parchment and I draw the features of the top of the volcano and the position of the flags. I'm complimented when he enters my drawing into the ship's log.

The next five days are uneventful, then an unusual storm takes us by surprise, an easterly wind head-on, and we set a course north by northeast which will carry us far off our normal heading, but nearer the North Pacific Drift, the stream that circles the whole Pacific in a clockwise motion. The Sandwich Islands are twenty degrees north of the equator, we enter the favorable stream around thirty degrees and San Francisco, our first port of call, is thirty-seven-degree latitude. We lose little heading northwest. That said, I'll bet we're reduced to three knots in speed when it comes to a true westerly course.

As the wind increases, it's more and more a call for all hands, until we finally face a Force Seven storm, winds over forty knots and reefed sails to twenty-five percent. No staysails are flying and even the jibs are one-fourth their normal exposure. And with all that, we're heeled so far to the larboard we eat sitting on the deck from bowls as nothing will stay on tilted tabletops. All grog is forbidden as the captain wants every man to be surefooted, as a man overboard means a man lost. Reversing course is a timely and dangerous task and even launching a jolly boat to attempt a recovery would likely mean loss of not only that man, but a jolly boat and its crew of four.

Finally, after a week of sea whipping into our faces, being wet and never fully dry even after hanging clothes for the alternate four hours we sleep, and no sight of the sun, the wind lets up and reverses to a sailor's delight. Pure joy she blows eighteen knots from out of the west, and we again are able to set full sail including staysails. We're nearly ten degrees north of our planned course but riding a favorable current that will soon take us southeast.

As much as I hate parts of this job, I've come to believe there is nothing more beautiful than a full three-masted ship with full sail pushing her onward. The crew is again singing chanteys as we work, and the first day under full sail happy as the captain has awarded us an extra measure of grog and instead of burgoo—mush and molasses—we enjoy salt fish and he even breaks into a case of mangos he'd hoped to reach port with, and cook prepares a mango pudding to rival the Niantic Hotel.

Due to the storm, we sight San Francisco in twenty-one days, the same as our voyage over, even with a following sea and fourteen days of favoring winds.

We dock on a high tide at three in the afternoon and begin off-loading. I only work an hour before Captain Constantine and I are summoned to the Niantic Hotel to meet with Lord Stanley-Smyth and then dine with him and his missus.

As we head for the gangplank, I pass Charley O'Donnell who, with three other men, is tending a sprocket winch, off-loading a pallet loaded with cane sugar.

He sings as we pass, "Monkey see, monkey do!" substituting the words into the chantey the whole work detail is enjoying.

It's all I can do not to stride over and slap his ears to

ringing, but I'm following the captain and that's my task at the moment.

But I file it away for future attention.

## 34

Lord Stanley-Smyth and his Lady seem happy to see me.

"Sugar is coming very dear here in the city and in the camps," he advises me. "Your share of the haul should be over four hundred dollars."

"Thank you, sir," I say, sincerely, then add, "but I feel I must head for the Columbia and to the Snake to check on my family."

"I expected that," he says. "Can't help but be disappointed but am not surprised. And if all's well at home, can we expect you back?"

"If I'm welcome, sir, odds are I'll be back."

"There's still this problem with the Wallabys. City Marshal Crozier has had feelers out all over the city. The man you shot in the leg lost it just below the knee, and he hasn't lost interest in you. The five-hundred-dollar reward for the head of Jake Zane still stands. The gang is now over fifty strong and the most powerful hooligan group in the city. The *Orient* is leaving for Mazatlán day after tomorrow, and the *Windsong* for another lumber run on the tide the next day. Your choice?"

"That's more than kind of you, sir. It's the *Windsong* and a one-way trip to as close to the Columbia as she sails."

"Then one way it is, young Jake."

The Lord has again gotten me a room in the Niantic, this time a garret on the fourth floor, not quite as fancy as my last one and a valet doesn't come to help me dress, but then I don't need to tie a four-in-hand.

Thinking the Wallabys will be on the lookout for a sailor, I retrieve my goods from the locker I've rented from the establishment and dress in my plains clothes—broad-brimmed hat, canvas pants, calf-high mule-skin boots, an elk skin pullover, my hunting knife on my left side in a beaded sheath I took off an Indian who no longer had use for it, and my Colt. I even hang my possibles bag over my shoulder. I guess I was tired of being a sailor for a while. I leave my scattergun and Sharps in the room, and since the Lord and his Lady have again set out for Sacramento on a side-wheeler, I am free for a night or two. And I plan to make good use of it. Mumu and Koa have invited me to a gathering of Sandwich Islanders in big meadow near Fort Presidio, where the few native women among them are to treat us with island dances and the men with pig roasted over open fires. After days of burgoo and dandy funk, I'm ready for a chunk of roasted meat.

I pull the hat low as Lord Stanley-Smyth has warned me I'm still a prime target for the Wallabys or anyone who'd like to fill their pockets with five hundred in gold after delivering my head to the now one-legged Ian Burnie, stud duck of the Wallabys.

As an added precaution I have a quiet beer in the

small bar of the Niantic and wait until the streets are only lighted by whale oil lanterns, then cross the street to hire a gig—feeling flush knowing I have a big payday coming—to take me around the harbor to the big meadow.

The good news is, the streets are even more crowded with gold-seeking pilgrims, money-grubbing, pilgrim-gouging, townsmen, and ladies of the night, than when I set sail for the islands over a month and a half ago. I yell at the hack driver, and he tips his hat and motions for me to mount up. Even as late as it is, I have to weave through wagons and drays loaded with beer kegs, passengers, loads of lumber, gravel and rocks, and all sorts of goods going to restock the markets. I swing up behind the gig driver just before another hopeful passenger swings up from the other side...and find myself face-to-face with the barrel-shaped Wallaby who was alongside Ian Burnie when I elected to shoot a leg out from under him.

"What the..." the man starts to say, his eyes wide with recognition. But I don't tarry and place the heel of my mule-skin boot in his chest, and shove. He windmills his arms and crashes flat on his back on the boardwalk.

"Go driver, before the lead flies!" I yell, tapping the drive on the shoulder with the barrel of my Colt. He gets the hint and the little paint horse pulling us is off with a leap. I watch carefully making sure the Wallaby doesn't try to pursue us, but he's having his own trouble.

The chunky Wallaby is trying to stand but grabs onto another big sailor in a striped shirt who takes offense and shoves him back hard. He's again flat on his back as the hack driver takes a turn and we're out of sight.

"Driver," I yell, "it's a half dollar you keep up the pace! I'm late for a haunch of roast pig." He nods without turning and pops the paint on the hindquarters with his long quirt.

I sigh deeply, the cab was just across from the Niantic and I'm wondering if when I return, I won't have fifty Wallabys surrounding the place, hoping to collect ten dollars apiece, sharing the five hundred posted on my head. It's said there are over thirty thousand souls in San Francisco and as many times as the good Lord has saved my hide in the last three years, I wonder if his patience is growing thin.

There will be time enough to worry on it. Now is time for some enjoyment with my large native friends.

When Mumu and Koa invited me, they said a family gathering. I guess when an islander says family, it's in the tradition of the word they'd taught me, *ohana*, or family in a much broader sense than I'm used to. There must be two hundred Kanakas gathered in the meadow around a half-dozen fires large enough to light up the night. And those half-dozen fires don't count three beds of coals, glowing bright under three slowly rotating hogs that must weigh over two hundred pounds before they began dripping and feeding fat to the fires below.

Koa and Mumu introduce me around, always keeping me between them, always following the introduction with the word *ohana*. I guess so all would know they consider me as close as blood. Near each turning pig is a hogshead barrel and I'm dipped a mug of brew. "*Okolehao*," Mumu says with that infectious grin.

I raise the clay mug to him and repeat, "*Okolehao*," having no idea what I'm saying, but presume it's a toast of some kind.

He laughs. "No, drink is *okolehao*, island drink for celebration. Drink down. You now *ohana*."

It's my turn to laugh. I guess this drink is the island

form of rum. I tip it up and he reaches over and with a big paw, raises it higher, laughs, and the liquid pours down my throat, alcohol hot as fire and strong as any rum or whiskey I've tasted.

Those all around me laugh and pat me on the back as Koa dips me another mug full. Luckily after the second mug I'm given the full rib of one of the big pigs. It's been dipped in some liquid concoction seemingly made from mangos and is delicious and dripping with goodness. My elk shirt is wet from my chin to my belt, but after the two mugs and with another full one in one hand and another rib in the other, I care little.

I haven't stopped laughing and smiling, drinking, and chewing, since I paid the cabby the fifty cents I promised, and a dime tip…that is until I see the half-dozen native women begin to dance to the rapid ring of an equal number of drums.

Searching for a word as I watch, but probably too tongue-tied to pronounce it, it finally comes to me: sensuous. All the girls have flowers in their hair and attached to each wrist. They are as graceful as swans for part of the dance, then nearly as rapid as hummingbirds for another. One of the girls in particular is bare in the midriff, her skirt only just below the knee and split up to midthigh, her hair hangs, shiny and thick, to a point that makes me wonder how such firm buttocks can wiggle so quickly.

I stand dead silent, mainly appreciative, as I take it all in. Even standing still and merely watching, the heat floods my loins.

Until Koa taps me on the shoulder and points back to the street some forty paces away. It's a gig and it's pulled off the street and up onto the grass.

"You schedule hack man?" he asks.

He's right, it's the same hack with the paint pony I hired to get here, only this time it carries the Wallaby who I shoved to his back. He's not alone as I recognize the big man with a peg leg who also drops to the grass. Behind him are four wagons loaded with men. At least two dozen Wallabys alight from the wagons and line up facing us.

The odds would be good, except all of the Australians are armed with shotguns and revolvers, clubs and knifes, and I bet there's not a half-dozen firearms among the whole mob of Kanakas.

Quickly the islanders realize something is amiss and the drumming stops and the two groups face each other in silence.

I guess it's my cue to act.

## 35

So act I do.

Some problems you just can't run from. I stride forward with purpose, pulling the Colt as I do. My arms extended and Ian Burnie is zeroed in my iron sights before any of them have time or feel the necessity to pull their weapons. I'm ten feet from him and stop. From my peripheral vision I realize both Koa and Mumu have paced me and are ten feet on either side.

"This is between you and I, you fat Wallaby coward," I yell at the top of my lungs.

"We'll shoot you to pieces," he says, taking a peg leg step forward. Then he looks from Koa to Mumu and screams, "Y'all got no dog in this fight. Leave."

But both of them take a step nearer the Wallabys, and the other Kanakas are beginning to move, and not away.

As I know from what Lord Stanley-Smyth has told me, the Wallabys are being watched closely by the city coppers, I'm even more relieved to see two paddy wagons pull up and instead of loading wrongdoers, they unload more than a dozen uniformed police who spread out behind the Wallabys and stand with revolvers in one hand and long hardwood nightsticks in the other.

I'm encouraged. I take another step forward and my eyes burn into Burnie's. "I promise, the first man fills his hand tells me without hesitation to put at least one in your fat gut. You all may shoot me to pieces, but not long after they'll be throwing dirt in both our faces. You want to die just because I do?"

As we're trading barbs the Kanakas are filtering around the gang of Wallabys, at first seeming as if heading for the street to leave, then I realize they've turned and are infiltrating the group. Most are weapon-free, but in easy reach of the Australians.

Ian swivels his head looking from side to side, realizing the odds are badly against them. I sense his surprise that the islanders have chosen to back my play.

"You ain't gonna ever be able to give me my leg back," he says, still with fire in his eyes.

"You lost a leg, fat man, but you gained a valuable lesson."

"What's that?" he says, looking a little puzzled.

"You're a big man, and I'm sure could easily take me in a fair fight, not that you've ever fought fair in your life. The lesson is, as Colonel Colt said, this tool I have in my hand makes all men equal, big, little, young, old. And another thing, three no-accounts with those walrus-handled blades y'all seem so proud of don't equal one fella not even reached his majority at the time. You need to go back to the hole you slithered out of and think on that."

He's silent for a minute, realizing that my new family is not backing down as now between every Wallaby are at least two Kanakas. And behind them watching this all transpire are over a dozen of San Francisco's finest.

"We're gonna settle this, punk," he mumbles.

"I can settle it right now, putting a slug of lead dead center through your heart, if you have one, and you know I hit what I aim at."

The barrel-shaped Wallaby I'd shoved down as he was getting into the hack steps forward. "There'll be another day, boss," he says.

I take a couple of steps closer as Burnie glances over at his mate. He glances back and I manage a half smile and drop the muzzle to his good knee.

"You know, I think sending you to hell might not be as good as making you live your miserable life out on two stubs."

"Hold on," he says, extending both hands out palms flat as if he can ward off my shot. It seems I've found something that he fears even more than dying. I can only imagine the agony a man goes through losing a limb and having to learn to negotiate without it.

"Listen to your friend, Burnie. A lot of men could die here this evening. You'll sure as hell's hot be one of them, and hell will be where you find yourself."

"This ain't over," he says, but spins on his one good leg and pegs away, yelling at his gang, "Another day, lads, another day."

And they are gone.

As we regroup around the roasting pigs, Koa and Mumu still at my side, I look from one to the other. "Family, *ohana*, is good, my new brothers."

They both laugh and dip another mug of *okolehao*. I turn to see City Marshal Robert G. Crozier and his band of city police walking up.

"Nice evening, Mr. Zane," he says.

"Yes, sir. It is now." I glance at Koa and Mumu. "Lots of pig?"

"Plenty," Koa says, laughs, and starts dipping mugs for the coppers.

It is sure as the devil a nicer evening than it might have been.

Now all I've got to do is worry about getting back to the hotel in one piece, and without two hundred family members backing me up.

## 36

It's well after the witching hour, and for the last three, without them seeing, I've managed to pour mugs of their strong liquor back into the hogshead barrels and can walk straight and hopefully see into the shadows as I try to return to my room. Return without coming face-to-face with a half-dozen shamed and angry Sydney Ducks. Wallabys. I suggest to both Koa and Mumu they leave the party with me but both are well into their cups and happy to be with their people. They'd likely not be much help and I'd be the shamed one if they were badly injured or killed due to their diminished capacity.

So I slip away into the woods, staying away from the permanent town buildings and weaving my way through trees and tents, most the canvas hovels now dark. I walk a full half mile south before I turn east into a neighborhood where fire-destroyed structures are being rebuilt. As is too often the case, the fog has rolled in and occludes moonlight. It's dark as deep in the bowel of the *Windsong*. As I move out of the construction area, I make sure not to wander down any streets with saloons or bawdy houses still roaring with crowds and keep to those dark lanes, without whale oil street lights or with the lights extinguished. I go a block past the Niantic's street and then a half block until I find the alley behind the four-story hotel, and make it to a back door and into a scullery, a room with iron sinks and counters now stacked with crockery and fine china. It's as quiet as a graveyard at midnight.

There's a man at the counter, but he's seated with his feet up on the desk and appears to be dozing, so I toe-heel it to the stairs and make my way four flights up to my floor.

I have no trouble sleeping.

Having a full day to kill and being on the Lord's poke I dress, have a leisurely breakfast in the hotel restaurant of something called quiche Lorraine, some egg, spinach, onion, and chunks of ham mishmash all on a crust a little like one of my ma's delicious apple pies. Dang if it ain't pretty as a French actress in a lace nightgown—I can say that as I saw one advertising a stage show when wandering the streets—and tastes as good as I would imagine she smells. I also have a plate of something they call French toast, not lathered with molasses but rather a thin syrup the waiter says comes all the way from Maine and is drawn from maple trees. And the little toasts are sprinkled with cinnamon, said to come from another tree. I like it and a glass of some drink they say is the juice of the orange. I don't much favor the coffee as it's very strong and served in china cups so thin you can almost see through them and you have to worry about the breaking every time you pick one up. And you can't get a finger in the wee little thing they call a handle. Hate to drop one as they are pretty as a mountain meadow with little flowers painted on the thin walls. All that said, the meal surely shames burgoo and dandy funk.

Even with that leisurely meal, longer than I believe I've ever taken to eat at one sitting, I still have twenty hours before I can report to the *Windsong* as she's due to dock on the high tide in the still, dark morning.

There's a small lending library in a setting room off the entry and greeting desk so I wander in to peruse the books and newspapers. Spending a few minutes with a *Leslie's Weekly* I learn that—now that I'm a sailor it's of interest—there's a new yacht race called America's Cup and a schooner-rigged yacht called the *America* got a late start due to a fouled anchor line, yet finished first and the New York Yacht Club took home the cup.

I laugh to myself pretty sure that crew didn't dine on burgoo.

And New York has a new newspaper called, of course, *The New York Times*.

Gold has been discovered in Australia...maybe some of these damnable Sydney Ducks will head for home?

And the Sioux tribe has signed a peace treaty. I both fought with and befriended many tribes both following my pa around Missouri and crossing the country without him. I truly hope this treaty is something that brings the Anglos and the Indians together but have my doubts that will ever happen. The Indians have a love of the land that's far different than the white man's love of ownership of the land. Indians don't understand a fence and for that reason alone, I question the lasting value of any treaty. I wish the Sioux luck, and hope Anglos' hair is spared.

I finish the latest *Leslie's Weekly* and find a book by an author who recently died, Edgar Allan Poe. It's one that looks interesting *The Black Cat*, and I decide to go back to my room and the garret window, far from the eyes of any Wallabys, and read the day away. It's a pleasure I haven't partaken of in many a month. My late breakfast means I won't be hungry for lunch, even on the Lord's poke. But I'll damn sure be ready for a so-called last supper before I report to the *Windsong* and Miss Su Lee Hong's basic bowls of rice, beans, mush, salt pork, salt fish, and that seeming staple of every sailing ship, molasses.

And a one-way trip to the Columbia River.

I dine, again amused by the term, write a long missive thanking the Lord and his Lady, leave it at the desk, and with a backpack full of my worldly belongings I set out. My Colt is on my hip, my scattergun in one hand, my Sharps in the other, as I wander through the alleys down to the waterfront. I actually look forward to seeing Captain Polkinghorn, First Mate McGillicutty, Sour John, Jack Pyle, my rhyming shipmate, the redhead Boston Bob, and the others. I'm sorry that my friends Mumu and Koa are left behind on the *Orient*.

Of course a group of Wallabys are loitering near Murphy's Saloon and Seafood, so I avoid going anywhere close and rather make my way, in the darkness, to the end of the only dock with a vacant space large enough to accommodate the *Windsong*, which I presume has been reserved for her arrival. A pile of canvas makes a great place to recline, doze, and stay out of the gunsights of the Sydney Ducks, whose raucous laughing I can hear in the distance.

I'm awakened by a group of longshoremen launching a pair of boats that will each accommodate six oarsmen and see the *Windsong* laying a couple of hundred yards out in the bay, sails all furled. She's skillfully worked her way between the many skeletons of ships moored there but will need a tow to the dock.

In less than an hour I'm reporting to Captain Polkinghorn, and am happy to say I'm welcomed, however as a common seaman as my second mate position is filled by one Silas McCracken. So this time it's a hammock, but that's fine with me as I'm on my way to see if I'm still welcome in Amalie's arms. She was bound for the Willamette Valley, and I plan to make my way there from as close as the *Windsong* will take me, which I've explained to Captain Polkinghorn, along with the fact I have Lord Stanley-Smyth's consent to jump ship whenever I so desire.

Luckily, we're only in port for two days, and I'm busy aboard so have no run-ins with the Wallabys, and am happy to wave goodbye to San Francisco and my one-legged enemy and his gaggle of Sydney Ducks. We sail through the narrow channel at three in the morning into a smooth sea and in four days are sailing due west to a lumber camp at the mouth of the Rogue River. Ellensburg was the site of placer mining but more importantly for the *Windsong*, rafts of logs were floated down the Rogue to be milled near the rough-and-tumble town. It was as far north as the *Windsong* would have to travel as there was more than a shipload of lumber.

I agreed to stay with the ship until fully loaded, then waved goodbye to new and old friends as she sailed away.

## 37

NOW, IT IS DECISION TIME.

Either try and catch another ship north up the coast to the Columbia, then southeast up the river to the town of Portland, then south up the Willamette River and valley until I located Amalie. Or as the lumbermen at the camp inform me, I can cross the mountains east along the Rogue River then north across a small range to reach the headwaters of the Willamette. That will mean buy a horse or mule, or both, and take my chances with the Indians and a thickly wooded mountain range I didn't know.

As we've bought a shipload of lumber, the owner of the camp welcomes me to supper along with a trapper, Oliver Harding, who'd just made the trip down the Rogue. The owner and his son and foreman have a decent cabin and Chinese cook. John Tyler Sansome, camp proprietor, is a rugged sort as is Tyler his grown boy. They enjoy hearing my tales of the Sandwich Islands and I take the opportunity to pick Oliver's brain about the trip I am to face, although in the opposite direction. He has come up the Willamette, over the pass, and down the Rogue. The Sansomes are kind enough to sell me a pair of mules for ten dollars each, and have their wrangler throw in a well-worn dragoon saddle, pack saddle, and paniers.

I am up with the sun, eager to attack the mountain and riverside trail, rough as it is.

As I take the reins of the molly mule I am to ride, the wrangler laughs and cautions me, "She bites like a rattlesnake and kicks like a stuck bullfrog. Don't let your guard down, son."

"She got a name?" I ask.

"Sarah, and the john mule is Offal. He's sweet as sugarcane syrup."

"Why the name Awful then?"

"Offal, not Awful. That scar on his side was once't a wound from a big ol' black bear and his guts were stickin' out. I shot that bear then I stuffed 'em back, sewed him up, and he got the name. No worry as he healed up good."

I mount and Sarah decides to test me right off, she bounces across the lumberyard, stiff-legged until she jumps a pair of thick cedar logs, landing stiff so I nearly go over her head, but hang on to the applause and hoorahs of the lumber crew.

I guess she decides I am fit to set her back and calms down. The wrangler is slapping his thighs and guffawing as I rein her back to take up the lead rope of my pack john mule.

"Tolt ya," he says, and guffaws again.

"Ha," I say, as if nothing has happened, and add, "she's smooth as calf slobber."

He laughs again and all the men who've been watching yell their goodbyes and without looking back I gig the molly up the north side of the Rogue and am soon out of sight into the thick timber.

The john mule trails like a dream, never once setting back trying to dislodge my arm from its shoulder socket.

The little company store has provided me with sowbelly and a sack of hardtack, a cone of sugar, salt, a pick and shovel, some fine line and fish hooks, and a small crosscut saw as the trapper, Harding, informed me the rainforest was thick as hog's hair in places. I also bought a steel and flint for starting fires and fifty feet of good hemp rope to stake out the critters and whatever. Leaving the deck of two ships I can do things with line that I hadn't thought of on the plains, however, my experience hauling wagons up and down steep slopes has also served me well.

This forest is unlike any I've seen before, wet, full of moss and ferns, thick, and damn steep in places. Seems there is a long-eared or great horned owl every two hundred yards, which speaks of lots of rabbits or other small game, which I hear scurrying in the underbrush but never see. Ofttimes I am more than one hundred feet above the river, which is well named as it is a rogue, and at times a wild one at that. It wouldn't do to have a misstep as the next step could be the last one in many places.

And it's a good thing I have the sowbelly as I see nothing of wildlife until late the third day, when the steep country has lessened on the lee side of the coastal mountain range. I kill a small doe and enjoy a roasted haunch and pause long enough to jerk the rest of the meat.

I see nothing of the savages the trapper has warned me to watch for; then again maybe they saw me and how well armed I am. In that god-awful thick country they could have been watching, unseen, from twenty paces.

The fact is I am happy not to see another soul. Having lived an elbow's reach from other men, smelling of sweat and what a diet of beans produces, for over three months. I relish the silence, the whisper of pine boughs, the wafting odor of pine and cedar, and the kiss of morning mist on my cheeks.

And the water, fresh, cold, better than any mug of grog.

Harding told me to turn north on my fourth day on the trail, when the Rogue is a quarter as wide as near the sea, and when I see a wide pass to the north. And I do so.

On the morning of the fifth day, I awake to find my john mule missing. At first I figure he's pulled his stake and wandered off in search of greener pastures, then, on a muddy bank, I see the track of a half-dozen unshod ponies. My unseen savages have likely watched me make camp and decided they could use my mules, either to ride or eat. Coming back to my molly, still tied, I realize she has blood on her muzzle, and I see a trail of blood across the grass.

It looks to me like some savage got a surprise when he reached to untie her and instead got an armful of sharp mule teeth. I get a laugh out of that, surprised I didn't awake as he must have yelled banshee-like. Molly and I had become familiar, and she'd only once tried to chomp down on my arm, getting a nose full of fist for the effort. We'd quickly come to terms. She wouldn't bite me, and I wouldn't flatten her snout.

I liked that john mule as well, and hope he isn't

destined to turn on a spit in some Indian camp. But there have been at least a half-dozen unshod horses ridden near my camp, and I decide it would be foolish to give up my hide trying to save his. My ma often told me, "Discretion is the better part of valor."

So, discretion it is.

## 38

I wish Offal well and the Molly, Sarah, and I are soon looking down at what must be the headwaters of the Willamette. It's north flowing, and that's the proper direction.

It's another day of easy riding down the slow Willamette before I come upon a tilled field and a beautiful stand of wheat. Then I see smoke wafting from the stone stacks of four decent log cabins in the distance. The river here is near fifty feet wide, rock filled, but I presume before long will prove to be navigable with canoe or raft.

A woman tending her garden, with four children playing nearby, sees me coming and I hear her yell for her man.

"Thomas, rider coming!" she shouts and lays her hoe aside and herds her children into the nearest cabin. Then she stands near the door with hands on hips, watching me approach. Her man exits a half-built barn and disappears into the cabin, then reappears with a rifle cradled in his arms.

I rein up seventy-five feet from them and call out, "May I approach?"

"Come peaceful and be welcome," the man calls back, and I do so.

"Beautiful stand of wheat," I say as I dismount.

"You've farmed?" he asks, as he approaches and extends a hand which I take and shake.

"I'm Jake…Jake Zane, recently from working the lumber ships but off a farm over on the Snake. Come up the Rogue. On my way downriver, then, hopefully, up the Columbia to the Snake to see how my ma and sisters are getting on."

He looks at me suspiciously. "You left your ma and sisters to fend for themselves?"

I give him a bit of a sour look. "No, sir. I left them with Ma's new husband and a friend big and tough as this mule. The locust got our crops and we needed some more seed money."

He shakes his head, then invites me inside. "We got coffee, should you partake?"

"Obliged."

We trade stories on getting to Oregon then I ask, "Came west on the same train as a lady, Amalie Engstrom, who was headed for the Willamette. Don't suppose you know where she lit?"

"Sorry, don't know of any Engstroms," he says.

Then the wife speaks up for the first time. "Thomas, wasn't that family…man, wife, and new child…I think they were the O'Tooles…wasn't her name Amalie? Unusual name, Amalie. I'm sure that was it. Met them down at the French Prairie Trading Post last year."

He shrugs. "Don't remember."

She laughs. "Like Hades you don't. When did you ever forget a comely lass like that."

He laughs but holds his tongue.

I'm a bit crestfallen but keep my disappointment to myself. "So, O'Toole is it. If that's the same Amalie." And I can't help but ask. "My friend had long blonde hair, sometimes she braided it in a single braid, near to her waist."

"Real pretty girl," the wife offers with a nod. "Blonde with a good wit and ready smile. Babe on her hip didn't slow her down a mite. Of course, she didn't have four young'uns like myself."

"'Course not," I agree.

Then I rise. "Appreciate the coffee and wish I could pay you back."

He replies quickly, I guess hoping I'd say just that. "Got a header for my barn door too dang heavy to handle alone. Help me hoist it up?"

"You bet."

We finish that task in a very few minutes, and I'm off again. I'll ask again about Amalie as I continue downriver but have little hope now that she's been pining away for me the last couple of years. I guess this is a fool's errand on my part.

It's another two days before I come upon the place known as French Prairie Trading Post. I inquire about Amalie Engstrom, and get the same Amalie O'Toole, who's at a slight bend in the river not two miles north.

The river here is wide enough for a boat or raft and I've soon negotiated a trade for a ten foot long by eight wide well-constructed raft with a deck box, mast, and small canvas sail…not that I'll need it on the river.

So, it's goodbye Sarah molly mule, hello raft. If I can keep her afloat, I'll make in one day what I made in three, and will soon arrive in Oregon City then in half a day at Portland on the Columbia.

Seeing little future in the visit, still I decide to stop at the slight bend in the river and seek out the whitewashed cabin a half mile up slope, which I'm told is the home of Amalie O'Toole.

She answers my rap on the door, and nearly drops the baby she has propped on her hip.

We stare at each other for a long moment before she mumbles, "Jake Zane..." then adds, "I'm married."

I can't help but laugh, before I say, "I should hope so, with that wee child on your hip."

"I'm sorry," she manages, "I just thought..."

"And I just thought I'd say howdy-do, just passin' by, and it would be rude not to."

"I'm sorry," she says again, and I don't know if she means sorry for being married, sorry for seeing me on her step, or sorry for leaving me there, then she adds, "come in, come in, where in the world are my manners."

But I don't move. "I didn't mean to intrude."

"Intrude, don't be a silly. Liam is out in the field but will be here for lunch soon. You have to stay...at least for lunch," she says, then blushes as red as the wild roses on either side of her step.

Liam is a burly bloke who obviously has never fought shy of the table, and like most Irishmen seems to live off potatoes. Only with the two milk cows I see in a nearby pasture, his are slathered in plenty of butter. He's a jolly sort, which pleases me as I quickly see Amalie is not only well thought of but well taken care of. After two bowls of venison stew, with of course plenty of potatoes and cabbage, Irish salt bread, and Liam and I polishing off half an apple pie, I take my leave. Leave with the promise to give Amalie's regards to my mother, sisters, and Sampson, the escaped slave who was my rock and ofttimes savior on the two-thousand-mile trek on the Oregon Trail.

When I leave to head back to the river, I don't look back. It seems I've closed a book on part of my life.

I float gently past the capital, Oregon City, maybe three dozen buildings with another half dozen under construction, without stopping, as I have the mighty Columbia in my sights.

Before reaching that goal, I'm somewhat surprised to have to head for a bank to avoid an oncoming side-wheeler, aptly named *Columbia*.

Now, former hopes somewhat dashed, in dead darkness, other than the lights of the two dozen buildings of Portland, I tie the raft to a pine sapling and sleep.

Tomorrow is another day, and the mighty Columbia River.

## 39

Come morning I wander the two streets of Portland taking in the sights. When there's a million acres of timber within sight, there's little need for stone buildings so most all the town is of whitewashed fine sawn lumber. It's a beautiful town, particularly considering as remote as it is. I've seen a half-dozen sawmills up and down the Willamette and spot another half dozen on the shores of the mighty river, most all that product bound for San Francisco. I soon learn I can travel east to rough water and falls known as the Cascades, on one of three side-wheelers. The *Columbia*, the *Jason P. Flint*, and the *Lot Whitcomb* each make the trip, then if lucky I'll catch a small sailed-and-poled river raft all the way up the Columbia then the Snake to Lewiston. It's said if I pole it will serve as my fare.

I treat myself to a café bear steak, three cackleberries, a pile of potatoes, biscuits, and coffee, for one-third the price it would be in San Francisco.

The trick, I'm told, is to greet the side-wheelers as they dock and offer your services as an experienced river man. Which I do, boarding the *Lot Whitcomb* as soon as the passengers depart. The first mate is on deck getting ready to supervise the off-loading of stone for fireplaces. I do not tell him my river experiences were when twelve to fourteen years of age on my father's flatboat on the Missouri but claim plenty of experience both river and sea. And I'm hired, and soon find myself returned to the boat with my personals in hand, and quickly off-loading heavy stones.

There's a new railroad with mule-drawn cars bypassing the Cascades, but I find it is at the proud cost of six bits per one hundred pounds, or a dollar a person, so I decide to hoof it the five miles around the Cascades and do.

I'm twenty days from the Cascades to Lewiston, arriving with very sore shoulders from working a pole near the shore, sleeping when only too dark to see obstructions, and eating beans, rice, and bony carp…and occasional catfish…taken by the ship's captain as we move along the river. Four of us have poled the thirty-foot-long flatboat three hundred miles.

Poling from the bow of the boat to the rear, striding past three others again to the bow, and poling again is not my idea of river life, nor nearly as interesting as sea life. In fact, it's downright boring and damn hard work. I thought I was developing muscle climbing the ratlines of a sixty-foot mast, but know, as I say goodbye to the crew in Lewiston, that my shoulders, back, biceps, and stomach muscles are hard as the hubs of hell.

It's noon when I disembark in Lewiston and I go straight to the mercantile and buy my mother and sisters ten yards of fine cloth, four bonnets—Sampson's wife gets one also—and five pounds of rock candy to share with all.

And I set out to see what's been made of my farm and theirs, and to see if I'm remembered after more than a year's absence.

It's a five-mile hike, but shank's mare is far easier than poling a heavy flatboat and I make the journey in two and a half hours. I stand on a little rise and look at over two sections of land, three hundred twenty acres of it mine, wheat waving, corn with tassels moving gently in the breeze, gardens near the log houses fully green and knee high. Most interesting is a new barn near my ma's place, built I'm sure by my sister's husband, Twist, Sampson, and my stepfather, Quint.

The first soul I see is my stepfather, Quint Haroldson, former dragoon captain, who now has shovel in hand and is working the headgate of a ditch, diverting water from the creek. He sees me coming, shading his eyes with a hand. Then waves and yells to the house over two hundred yards away. I'm pleased when he throws the shovel aside and jogs to meet me, throwing an arm around my shoulder as my own true father would have done.

"Your mother has been pining for you, Jake. It's fine you're home."

My mother is speechless but throws both arms around me even before I can drop my pack and rid myself of scattergun and Sharps. She's sobbing too much to talk, and when I spread five hundred dollars in gold coin on her plank kitchen table, she sobs even more.

We talk for hours. Willy my younger sister is shy and a little standoffish, but my older sister and her husband, Twist, Sampson and his wife, Mary, embrace me. It's a welcome home party.

I don't spoil it by telling them I'm headed out again for San Francisco.

That can wait until the newness of my being home wears off.

There are three new farms, claimed by others, within a couple of miles of our places. So, for plowing, planting, and harvest there are six men helping out, as many as six men following mules for plowing makes the task go quickly.

I have no problem convincing the men that I should return to make sure we have gold to buy seed and plow shares and all else needed, just in case we have another crop failure or infestations of lotuses or whatever calamity might befall a farmer.

Convincing my ma is not quite so easy.

She shames me into waiting until after the harvest, so it's October 1st before I catch a flatboat all the way to the Cascades, this time having to pay as polers are not needed with the current. But downstream from the Cascades I do convince the first mate of the *Columbia* to hire me on, promising to stay employed until all cargo is off-loaded in Portland.

Then it's another lumber ship, the *Portsmith*, a gaff-rigged schooner, all the way back to San Francisco. And even with the late season, it's a pleasant journey even working as a common seaman and sleeping in a hammock.

We dock at midday with the help of something new to me, a steam driven side-wheeler only thirty feet long, called a tug for obvious reasons as she tugs us to, then pushes us aside the dock.

I've been months away from the still growing city but can only wonder if my indiscretion blowing a leg off the boss of the Sydney Ducks has been forgotten. I'm sure not as it would be hard for a fellow to forget one who cost him a leg.

## 40

So I wait until nightfall before I take my leave of the *Portsmith*—my armory in hand—and head to the Niantic Hotel, praying that Lord and Lady Stanley-Smyth are in residence.

And, luckily, I find him sipping an after-supper brandy in the hotel's library. He rises and gives me a smile, and to my great pleasure, an embrace as if I'm a long-lost son.

"I'm glad you're here," he says. "I have another adventure for you."

"But…" I start to say, and he interrupts me.

"You have mail, from the Sandwich Islands. I was about to send it on to Lewiston…"

"Thank God you didn't," I say. "May I see it?"

"It's being held at the desk."

"May I be excused for a moment?"

"Of course. I'll be right here."

I hurry to the desk, and as I suspected and hoped, the letter's sender is Miss Nancy Ann Tannenbaum. I move to a quiet corner beside a potted palm, that reminds me of the islands, and with some trepidation use my folding knife to open the letter.

> Dear Jake:
> I hope this finds you well. I'm writing to tell you how much I enjoyed our short friendship and to let you know I've met a wonderful young man. A minister, like my father. Tall and handsome like you. We are betrothed and will marry at Christmastime. We hope you'll come visit us wherever in the islands we're stationed. With great affection,
> Your dear friend,
> Nancy Ann

It's a short missive and has again proven my ma correct. She's often told me you should know a lady a year before you allow smitten to become something more. Even thinking about her good advice, I feel a little like I've been kicked in the stomach. Twice in the last couple of months. It seems the ladies don't remember me much after I'm gone. I wonder if this is what fickle means. That said, maybe I'm the fickle one as there is supposed to be only one true love, and I've been smitten by two. Then again, maybe I'm often gone too quickly and too far to be remembered? Out of sight, out of mind, seems the order of this year in my life. Smitten suddenly seems too much like bitten.

Then again, if I return to the farm, there's not another eligible young woman, at least to the best of my knowledge, for three hundred miles in any direction.

I refold the letter and place it in the pot beside the trunk of the potted palm and return to where Lord Stanley-Smyth has taken a seat and is reading.

He glances up, takes a sip of brandy, then asks, "I'm

sure you've never been to England. I'm called home and the missus and I require a bodyguard for the trip, particularly across the isthmus. Then, after visiting our estates in Ireland, possibly on to St. Petersburg."

"St. Petersburg?"

"Russia. I presume you've never been to Russia?"

I look a little dumbfounded, so he continues, "It's ten dollars a day—day in, day out."

My math is pretty good, and unless the price of wheat and corn goes through the roof...

What the hell.

## A LOOK AT: SHADOW OF THE MAST

### BY L.J. MARTIN

**From the author of Two Thousand Grueling Miles and Rugged Trails comes a saga as wide and wild as the Americas.**

From Boston to Old California, young Sam McCreed grows to become as hard and skilled as the friends and foes he works alongside and escapes into a land equally threatening and dangerous as the watery hell that brought him to her shores. A young man now hardened by fists, ice, sea, and lash, he escapes into a California that has become a caldron boiling over with danger and resentment. And McCreed, now an unequaled horseman, an expert with blade, musket, and reata, is a man on the prowl for vengeance.

Driven by a lust and love for a fiery-eyed, raven haired senorita, he'll send any man who stands in his way straight to hell.

*AVAILABLE NOW*

# ABOUT THE AUTHOR

**L. J. Martin** is the author of 70 young adult, classic western, historical and thriller novels with a half-dozen non-fiction works among the mix. His first novel was a Y.A. and is still in print. As the father of four boys he was adamant about them filling their days with good books, books that taught values and how great the American experience is and was. He lives in Montana on a small ranch and winters in Prescott, Arizona, both homes in western areas steeped in history. Having wrangled, packed mules, farmed and ranched, sailed his own ketch, and studied history all his life, he's particularly suited to writing about what he loves, the west. He's lived among and studied its critters, ranchers, miners, soldiers, mariners, river men and townsmen and women, and their history. His most recent historical endeavor was writing/directing/producing the classic western film EYE FOR EYE, adapted from his novella of the same name..